Dance Around The Dandelion

Dance Around The Dandelion

DIMA BADER

atmosphere press

For Lina Drubi, who always kept
the faith even when mine wavered.

"Beautiful as a dandelion-blossom,
golden in the green grass, this life can be."

~Edna St. Vincent Millay

"Be like a dandelion, whenever they fall apart,
they start again, have hope."

~Anonymous

Part 1

THE FIRST FAMILY

CHAPTER 1

Sameer, 1962

Sorrow is slippery, crafty, and cruel. It sometimes acts coy and allows us to hope, imagine, and envision a life free of its clutches. Only then, after it ensures a modicum of happiness has entered, does sorrow descend to finish what it had started.

Sameer's line of thinking was occupied. He was rationalizing, evoking different memories, trying not to listen to the man in the white coat.

"We are getting good reports about Vincristine; it's a new drug, but I am hopeful..."

Sameer, a man of very few words at the best of times, sat dumbstruck and silent. He stopped paying attention after the word 'hopeful,' although he's fairly sure five or six other words succeeded. His wife, Lubna, sat beside him in the utilitarian office. The last time they sat on this exact sofa, about a year and a half ago, in front of this same doctor, they had received good news, excellent news, in fact. They were told that their daughter Faten was in remission and that her bone marrow was back to working properly. After several cycles of treatments, after losing her hair, after losing almost half her original weight and becoming a ghost of her previous self, after spending sleepless nights retching and shivering in one, or sometimes both, of her parents' arms, her bone marrow had finally started producing normal blood cells instead of only one type of defective cells.

Unlike her husband, Lubna was not a quiet woman; she

had questions, she was angry, wanted to lash out, wanted to exact punishment on whatever and whomever had caused this.

"We have never missed a check-up appointment. We have done everything like you said, every test and every exam. Faten was doing great; her last exam was not two months ago. They said she was doing well, she was healthy. What happened?! What did we do wrong?"

"You did nothing wrong. First, she was doing well, now she's not. These things happen. It's called a relapse..."

"I know what it's called!" she snapped at him. "I know what a relapse is." Then, her voice calmer but still reproachful, "I want to know why?"

"It happens. I'm sorry, and I know it's a difficult time for you. I understand what you are going through..."

"No, you do not!"

"About fifteen percent of children treated for acute lymphoblastic leukemia who achieve remission will have a relapse. It's no one's fault and certainly not yours."

Silence prevailed in the room. Sameer was diligently inspecting a crack in one of the floor tiles. Lubna's teeth were meticulously working on her cuticles.

Minutes passed. The parents, regardless of temperament, were both resigned. The doctor carried on, "Like I said, this new drug is promising, reports are favorable, and we will start the treatment as soon as Faten's lab and bone marrow aspiration results are back."

***

Everything happened too fast. Faten was doing so well, they even dared to start planning again for the future, for holidays and birthdays and graduation.

Big House was experiencing a period of festivities. Suad was getting married in less than three weeks. Her friends, much like Suad herself, were rowdy and over at Big House almost daily since the date was set. Every evening, the girls would congregate in Suad's room under the pretense of helping her arrange and pack her belongings in preparation for the move to her new home, and the reality was they were using this as an excuse to dance, eat, and laugh until late into the night, later than they're typically allowed to stay out, but not too late that eyebrows would be raised. The parents of the young ladies knew the formidable *Um Sameer*, whom all respected and admired, and none of them opposed her chaperonage of their daughters. *Um Sameer* was thrilled over the boisterous bunch, although she might not have been too obvious in parading her delight. She had no objection to them coming over every evening, and her only condition was that her daughters, her twins and the bride-to-be, who were still living at home, would clean everything up after their guests had left and return the house to its spick-and-span status before they went to bed each night. Her girls agreed, and each carried out her chores thoroughly so as not to be deprived of the recurring celebrations.

Faten heard of the festivities in her grandparents' house and begged her mother and father to take her there. "Please, Mama, just once. I just want to see what they're up to. I'm sure it's so much fun. Please. Please. Please!"

"*Habibti*, my love, are you sure? There won't be girls there your age. You'll get bored."

"Bored! No way. Besides, Mama, have you forgotten that Aunt Feryal and Aunt Fatima are only four years older than me? Please!"

"Ok, we'll ask *Baba* to take us tomorrow evening to Big House."

Tomorrow came, but when the time came to go, Faten said she wasn't feeling well. Lubna told her to go lie down for half an hour, and if she wasn't better by then, there was always tomorrow. Half an hour passed and then a full hour, and Faten didn't feel any better. By the next day, Faten developed a high body temperature. By the evening, the fever had spiked. Alarm bells started to go off when Lubna noticed faint bruising on Faten's thighs in the days following.

***

Mona and Laila, Sameer's sisters who lived in the United States, were scheduled to come home to attend their younger sister's wedding in a week. A year and a half previously, and after Faten's diagnosis, Sameer and his wife and daughter had traveled to the United States and stayed at Laila's home in Houston while Faten was treated at the Texas Children's Hospital.

After the recent fever and the bruising, and following an abrupt emergency consult, the overwhelmed parents were told that the cancerous blood cells had returned. Stupefied by the news, Sameer made what he thought at the time, and under the circumstances, the only rational decision: to return to Houston.

"Please, Mother, I beg you, don't telephone them." His tone, tired and drained of emotion, revealed that this conversation was the last thing in the world he wanted to be having at this moment. "There is no need for the girls to know."

While he was loath to do so, Sameer had to share the bad news with his parents. The twins were inside, and Suad was out with a friend on a last-minute spree in preparation for her upcoming nuptials, so the three of them sat around the table in the kitchen.

"The doctors have assured me that Faten could receive her treatments here, but I feel that going back to Houston will be better. For her to see her original doctors, they know her case better..." Sameer trailed off, not knowing what to say anymore. He just wanted this nightmare to end.

"That's why I should ring Laila and Mona. How will you manage in America alone?" *Um Sameer* said, still insisting that her daughters should know. She felt trapped; she wanted to help her son but didn't know how.

"Mother, please, I beg you," Sameer repeated his earlier appeal. "There is no need. I won't get lost in Houston! The only thing you'll be doing is spoiling the girls' fun, and there is nothing they can do for me there. We will manage."

"But..."

His father interjected, "No buts, Roqaya. He is right. It is bad enough that her brother won't be at her wedding. Think of Suad; her wedding will go ahead as scheduled. There is nothing we can do about it. So leave it at that."

There were very few people that could render *Um Sameer* silent. In fact, there were only three: her parents, both deceased, and her husband.

Abu Sameer was a man of few words, a trait his only son had inherited and perfected. As long as *Abu Sameer* did not speak, his wife reigned supreme in their home and among their acquaintances. But, conversely, his word was final; *Um Sameer* had learned a long time ago that the finality of her husband's words was not to be tested.

"They are bound to notice that their brother is not around. What do we tell them then?" she asked.

"Delay telling them as long as possible," Sameer answered his mother. "And when you can't keep the news any longer, tell them we're there for a check-up and not that the cancer is back. Then, after the wedding, maybe... hopefully, I'll have better news by then..." Sameer rested his head in his hands and wept.

On that late autumn afternoon, while the three of them sat around the kitchen table in Big House, neither mother nor father knew how to console their only son, so they looked at each other impotently because nothing could prepare a parent to deal with this kind of tragedy—the sickness of a helpless child and the hopelessness that ensues from carrying such a burden.

***

The only one who raised any formidable objection to the plan was Faten herself. She demanded to know why it was so necessary to go right now on a trip before she was to see her Auntie Suad dressed in white. And what about the dress that *Um Ahmad* had labored over especially for her? And all the hours spent on the intricate beading of the bodice will be wasted if she doesn't get to wear it.

She begged and she pleaded with her parents, "Can't we wait for another ten days, *Baba*, please?"

It seemed like a reasonable request; what were ten days in the scheme of things? But the problem that both her parents noticed, but neither was willing to express out loud nor acknowledge to the other, was the rapidity of their daughter's health deterioration. She had been lethargic and experiencing increasing joint pain that worsened each day since the fever began about a week ago. Even while arguing her case, she had difficulty breathing.

The trip was set for two days hence. Theirs was a long and arduous itinerary; they would travel from Amman to Beirut and thence to the States via London. Sameer tried unsuccessfully to use Faten's love for flying as an incentive, but to no avail. Instead, Faten threw a terrible tantrum as a last resort to make her parents see it from her point of view.

"It is so unfair; please, Mama, I'll be good, I promise," she had told them. Sensing that this whole upheaval in her life was connected to her health issues, she added while lifting her forehead so her father could check her temperature, "I'm feeling better already, *Baba*."

It ripped them apart and added to their misery. Her anguish sliced through their beings. Telling her no was the most difficult thing either had ever experienced.

Decades later, in another life, Sameer would tell another daughter about the day he refused Faten her last wish. He would explain how it felt when his heart was torn in two and how, with every passing day, the tear grew deeper, not shallower, and the pain got worse, not better.

9

CHAPTER 2

Lubna, 1963

Excerpts from the counseling session transcripts between Mrs. Lubna B. and Dr. Hussein Ezzat.

Kuwait City, Kuwait, 1963

Thursday, May 16th

L.B.: She's no longer here. She's no longer with me. I don't understand it. I can't understand how something like this could happen to someone so young, so beautiful, so innocent... That I'll never get to see her again or talk to her again or have her in my arms again. I don't understand how it happened. I don't know how I'm going to live now. What am I supposed to do now? Why am I supposed to stay alive? Why?! Life is not supposed to be this way. It's just not right. I am so angry. It feels... I don't know how to express it...

H.E.: Then don't, not right now; take your time, Lubna.

L.B.: I can't cry. I cried once. When they took her from my arms, you know, after... She looked so peaceful, as if she was sleeping, and they came, and they took her, and I screamed at them. I fought them, but after that, no more tears, not even one drop.

Wednesday, May 22ⁿᵈ

L.B.: I'm so tired. I'm tired all the time. I'm also so nervous. All the time...

H.E.: Tell me more about what makes you nervous, Lubna.

L.B.: I don't know how to explain it.

H.E.: Take your time. We're not in a hurry. Whenever you are ready.

L.B.: I'm anxious that I haven't dreamed of her, not once since she left me. I want to see her. I think it's because of the pills. I want to stop them. Please! I want to stop taking them. You know, the last ones you prescribed.

H.E.: The pills are to help you sleep and make you less anxious.

L.B.: But I feel the pills are making me too drowsy. I can't think. I can't concentrate. I want to remember, not forget. Please, Doctor Ezzat...

H.E.: Lubna, you can stop taking them if you want to. However, I suggest that we try lowering the dose and see what happens. How about that?

Wednesday, May 29ᵗʰ

L.B.: I don't know what more I could have done. We never missed an appointment or skipped a test. Never. The doctors assured us that all the tests were accurate, but the cancer suddenly came back, and nothing could have been done. I can't accept that. There must have been something that should have been done but wasn't.

H.E.: I understand that Faten was treated in one of the best facilities. Tell me about your husband, Lubna. This is our third session together, and you haven't mentioned him.

L.B.: No... I...

H.E.: It's alright, if you don't want to talk about him now, we can speak of him later if you wish. Let us talk about Faten, then.

L.B.: She was so brave. So brave trying to hide the pain. Until almost the very end, my baby insisted that she was tough.

Tuesday, June 4th

L.B.: We left Amman with Faten in somewhat unusual circumstances. Extraordinary, I might call them. You see, Faten wanted so much to stay for her aunt's wedding, she was so looking forward to it, *habibti*. We knew that she should start treatment as soon as possible. There was no time to waste. Faten, my love, I don't think she forgave us. She wouldn't talk to me, or to her father, all the way to the States! I cajoled, and I sweet-talked and made promises that I won't be able to keep because she's... gone... Excuse me...

H.E.: It's quite alright, Lubna. There's a box of tissues next to you. It is ok to cry.

L.B.: I'm sorry... I...

H.E.: No need to apologize. Take your time, and we'll continue whenever you're ready.

L.B.: She's gone now, and I feel... It feels like there is nothing for me anymore. She was my life, and now I'm without one.

H.E.: Let us talk about your husband. How did all this affect him? Have we discussed the possibility of group therapy?

L.B.: He's not here... in Kuwait. I'm here visiting my family... alone.

H.E.: I understand that for now. I am suggesting the possibility that in the future, both of you can benefit from group therapy.

L.B.: The doctors said she was responding well to the treatment. It was a new drug that they were using, and the side effects were worse than when she had been there a year and a half earlier. But, like I said, the doctors told us that the new drug stopped the cancer cells. But then she got an infection... in her lungs... pneumonia. She had no immune cells in her blood. And then the antibiotics were not enough...

H.E.: It is alright to cry, Lubna. Take a deep breath. I'm here. Take your time.

L.B.: The antibiotics were not enough to fight off the infection. And she became so weak that they had to stop the cancer treatment too. Sameer became silent. It's like he shut down. He stopped talking to everyone; me included. When the doctors came to speak with us about what was happening, he wouldn't speak to them. He never asked a question or even made a comment.

H.E.: Do you see a different outcome had he not, to use your phrase, shut down?

L.B.: No, I don't. I'm not blaming him, if that's what you're asking.

H.E.: Tell me, Lubna, how would you have liked your husband to have acted under the circumstances?

L.B.: I don't know. I'm just sad. So sad.

Monday, June 10ᵗʰ

L.B.: I keep thinking of her. Everything reminds me of her. Every word uttered by anyone around me reminds me of when she said that exact word or talked about that same subject.

H.E.: How does that make you feel, Lubna?

L.B.: She sometimes said the funniest things, my Faten. She made us all laugh. She had an incredible sense of humor. She was a favorite of her grandparents and aunts in Amman. And when we used to visit here, she was my parents' little princess. *Habibti*, I miss her so much... I'm sorry...

H.E.: Do not apologize. Take your time.

L.B.: It's so senseless. A senseless loss. I can't comprehend it. I don't understand how this could happen. She was an innocent child. *Hayati*, my precious love.

H.E.: Lubna, the loss of a child is an unthinkable experience and a nonsensical ordeal. You are grieving. You are entitled to this time of grieving. There is no time limit to your grief, and there are no rules. You will have to make the rules as you go along. I am here to listen to you and guide you, as long as you want me to along this path, but ultimately, it's your journey to make.

L.B.: I feel helpless. At a loss. I feel that I'm repeating myself to you every time I'm here.

H.E.: Like I said, there are no rules. You can repeat yourself as much and as often as you like. But if I can make a suggestion, don't avoid talking about Faten. Always talk about the positive memories, keep them alive. I want to hear more about Faten's sense of humor.

Sunday, June 16^(th)

H.E.: Lubna, today, if I may, I want us to talk about your husband. How did Faten's father handle this ordeal?

L.B.: I mentioned his shutdown... He stopped talking to me, but not just me, everyone. He only spoke to Faten when she was awake. When the doctors wanted to talk about Faten and what was happening, he just listened, or it seemed he was listening, but I don't really know if he heard anything. We never talked about it then... or since. Then when she got pneumonia and stopped her chemo, the pain became horrible, and my darling couldn't keep up the brave front anymore. So they started her on strong painkillers... I'm sorry I can't talk about the last days without crying...

H.E.: Don't apologize, Lubna. Take your time. There are tissues next to you.

L.B.: She was sleeping most of the time in the end, and the few times when she was awake and with tolerable pain were very short. We wouldn't leave her side during those precious moments. Sameer was always at her bedside, murmuring to her how much he loved her and how sorry he was... He was a broken man. Then when my baby passed away...

H.E.: Take your time, Lubna. Would you prefer if we talked about something else?

L.B.: No, it's alright, Doctor Ezzat. When my baby passed, they let us be with her to say goodbye, and later when they took her from my arms, I became hysterical, I confess...

H.E.: That's understandable. And your husband?

L.B.: Sameer, on the other hand, turned stoic. He worked like a machine. I never saw him like that, not ever. He insisted that my Faten fly back with us to be buried in Amman. It wasn't an easy task—a lot of arrangements and paperwork, you know... He didn't ask for my opinion, although if he had, I would have agreed, of course. I think he was busying himself to hide his devastation.

H.E.: And during this difficult time, did you two communicate at all?

L.B.: Not at all. Nothing. Our last days in Houston were particularly hard. The heartbreak was unimaginable. I can't put it into words; it's so difficult. I tried to reach out to him but got a few grunts back, and that's all. The journey back was horrendous. Sameer's father, and my father, and my brother Waleed were at the airport to meet us in Amman. My father, and mother, and brother had flown to Amman and had beat us there when they heard the news. The next few weeks passed in a haze. The burial, mourning, and heartache... Can I not go into details about that time, Doctor Ezzat?

H.E.: Of course, if it's too painful. We agreed, your journey, your rules.

L.B.: Through all the sorrow and the pain at the time, I felt sorry for Suad, Sameer's younger sister, a newlywed in mourning. And his youngest twin sisters, who were just a few years older than my Faten, anyone could see the bewilderment on their faces. Everyone was as if hit on the head. All of us were walking in a daze.

H.E.: And during this challenging time, Lubna, who were the people that you reached out to for support?

L.B.: I didn't. I wanted to be alone.

H.E.: That's understandable. Sometimes people who are grieving want time for themselves, but other times they require closeness and companionship.

L.B.: I wanted to be alone. But during the first few days after my baby's funeral, everyone gathered in Sameer's family home. Hordes of people came and went to pay their respects. And I couldn't avoid them, although all I wanted was to be left alone; I didn't want to see anyone or talk to anyone. But in the evenings, I demanded to go to my house, and my mother stayed with me there. I have no idea where my father and brother stayed during that period, and I didn't ask. So I slept in my baby's room, and my mother left me in peace. She made sure I ate, and sometimes I would hear her come into the room to check on me, but she never spoke, and I appreciated that.

H.E.: Where, if I may ask, was your husband during that period?

L.B.: I honestly don't know where he spent the nights. His days were spent in Big House—that's his family's home, we call it Big House. Anyway, Big House was full of his sisters and their brood, who came from all over, the eldest two from Saudi Arabia and the middle two from the States. They came for Suad's wedding, and I guess were planning to spend time with their mother and father in Amman. But, maybe, when they heard the news about Faten, they changed their plans to stay longer. I don't know, I'm not clear on the specifics. But like I said, Sameer in the days stayed in Big House, because mourners were coming and going; at night I don't know where he went.

H.E.: Did you talk to him during the mourning period?

L.B.: I saw him fleetingly a few times in Big House. One time, I called his name, and he replied with a quick nod of the head and some unintelligible words, and that was it. The men occupied the guest room in the front of the house, and the women in the sitting room in another part of the house. Our paths didn't cross much.

H.E.: What about after the mourning period? Was there any communication between you two?

L.B.: A few weeks later, his sisters left. The ones that lived outside Jordan, that is. The ones married but living in Amman would often come to the family home during the day but go to their homes at night. Big House emptied out but for my in-laws and the twins. I stopped feeling the need to be there and started spending the days in my house. My mother and father also went back to Kuwait, and so did Waleed. My mother wanted to stay behind, but I insisted that she leave with them. I think she was heartbroken because I didn't need her. I promised to visit her soon in Kuwait. At the time, it was an empty promise that I didn't know if I would keep, but I made it anyway...

H.E.: If you'd like us to stop, Lubna, we can.

L.B.: It's ok. If we still have time, I would like to get this off my chest now. It's not a topic I want to open again. If you don't mind.

H.E.: Not at all. We still have time. Whenever you're ready.

L.B.: Sameer started to spend the nights in our house. I still stayed in Faten's room, and he remained in the main bedroom. We still didn't talk. To be honest, I didn't try to talk to him. And he, at that point, wasn't doing much talking to anyone, much less to me. As the days sped by, we became even more distant. A point came when I felt that even if we wanted to communicate, neither of us knew how or where to start. It felt hopeless. Then I decided to come here. The idea came out of the blue. I don't know how to explain it; it's as if something was pulling me to this city. I found him sitting in the living room, and I told him with no introduction. I just informed him that I was booking a ticket to Kuwait. I might have felt a hesitation in his features, a need to say something, but I was beyond caring about what he thought or what he wanted at that point. I just wanted to escape. It didn't feel that I was abandoning Faten or leaving her behind, and it still doesn't. I have her here in my heart and mind. I sleep with her stuffed elephant—it still smells of her... can we stop now? Please.

Monday, June 24th

H.E.: People who experience grief will benefit greatly from having a support system, Lubna. It is one of the coping strategies to help you deal with your loss. This support could be in the form of a family member or a friend. You can call this someone your anchor or pillar, the person who will ground you and help you along your path.

L.B.: Are you talking about Sameer?

H.E.: No, not specifically. But now that you have mentioned him, your husband can be your anchor, and you his. When you decide to return to your life in Amman, never underestimate the stability that an anchor can provide in this difficult time.

L.B.: The pain we've both experienced and are still experiencing is indescribable, Doctor Ezzat. It's too much for our marriage to bear.

H.E.: Like I have mentioned in our previous sessions, Lubna, you and your husband both will benefit greatly from sitting with a therapist and discussing all your issues together.

L.B.: Doctor Ezzat, I don't want to go back to Amman soon or ever.

CHAPTER 3

Sameer, 1963

It was during the long, sleepless nights that doubt seeped into Sameer's mind and did its absolute worst. Doubt in his actions, and doubt in his silence that, at the time, he thought he was keeping for the right reasons. The sorrow he felt during Faten's last days was so fierce that it threatened to consume him. He believed that the best way to prevent the sadness from turning into anger was to remain quiet. He was frightened that he might scare his wife, and he was terrified that she would see a side of him that he didn't want her to see, so he kept silent.

After weeks of doubt-doused nights, clarity started to dawn. He hadn't supported Lubna during the worst time of their lives, and he didn't let her help him, although he needed her more than she could possibly know. Instead, he had simply shut her out. By losing their baby daughter, he had lost his ability to prioritize. During those horrible weeks, he thought that everything else took a back seat to the tragedy that was transpiring in front of him. He hadn't grasped then, as he does now, that she too was losing her baby and that she too felt the gut-wrenching sorrow.

Since the very first time he set eyes on Lubna, he had felt a kind of peace come over him. Every time he rested his sights on her, that original feeling would reignite itself, and a sense of calm would envelop him, and he would bask in her presence and beauty.

That last day she was with him, the day she had told him

she was going to Kuwait, at that moment, he realized that maybe Lubna didn't understand what she meant to him—that perhaps she didn't appreciate how much he needed her. Her aloofness summoned a dread that he was about to lose her. He wanted to tell her, right there and then, all that he was thinking—to beg her to reconsider and stay with him. He wanted to explain that he was sure they could pass this difficult time together and that he was lost when they lost Faten, but if she left him now, he would be finished. He wanted to say all those things, but the words to carry out all this explaining eluded him. He was always under the impression that Lubna, of all people, understood him totally. Understood him more than anyone else he knew. He believed that she, by just looking into his face, knew what he was thinking and how he was feeling. Indeed, this was part of his attraction to her from the very beginning. Only at that moment, when she told him she was leaving, did the idea that he might have been mistaken for all those years enter his mind. Just then, he started to realize that this belief might very well be unfounded. That he took her understanding of his whims and moods for granted—that it was a picture he drew of Lubna in his mind that had no likeness of Lubna in reality.

And yet, while she was packing her things and preparing to leave, he still tenaciously clung to his idealistic image of his wife. He reevaluated the situation and persuaded himself that it was only a visit to her parents, after all. They were both grieving, and if she went to be with her mother for some time, that would be good for her and, ultimately, for both of them. She must know how he felt about her; even if he rarely spoke the words, she must know. So, he didn't argue the matter, and he didn't ask her not to go. He didn't tell her he needed her and wouldn't be able to go on without her. He didn't describe how his life would be meaningless without her. However, he did decide silently that after a few weeks had passed, he'd go to Kuwait City himself, and there, he would tell her all. He'd find the words and the way to make her see.

And so, Lubna left, and then the days passed one by one, and Sameer did nothing. And then weeks came and went, and he didn't follow her to Kuwait. Then a month and then two passed, and still, he made no move. This procrastination only added to his anxiety. Every day that elapsed made the prospect direr, the insomniac nights longer, and the punishing doubt heavier. On more than one occasion, during the months that Lubna was absent from his life, he had picked up the telephone to call her parents' house in Kuwait to ask to speak to her. He sat alone in his house in the dark, gazing into the receiver in his hand, listening to the dial tone emanating from it, and every time he reconsidered this action and aborted the attempt prematurely.

***

Abu Sameer owned a fabrics and textiles store in downtown Amman, a prosperous family business handed down to him from his father before him. His right-hand man, Sameer, was an intricate part of the smooth running of their trade. Near the middle of June, and after Sameer missed three days straight of work, *Abu Sameer* dispatched his wife to check on their son. Armed by her twins on either side, *Um Sameer* marched the fifteen-minute walk from Big House to Sameer's house and knocked on the door.

Anticipating that the door wouldn't be answered either because the sole occupant wouldn't be at home or maybe wouldn't want to answer, *Um Sameer* had brought with her the spare key that Sameer had given her before his departure to Houston months earlier and which she didn't give back because of the upheaval that followed. Her suspicion was correct, and after a few minutes had passed with the door unanswered, *Um Sameer* let herself in.

The squalid state of the house didn't surprise her. Clutter

of every kind, clothes, dirty cups, plates, empty bottles, and newspapers were strewn on the floor, the chairs, and every other surface. *Um Sameer* shot a sideways glance at her daughters, who were standing and staring with their mouths agape. Without further prompting, the twins scurried and busied themselves, tidying, dusting, and scrubbing to restore a semblance of normalcy to their surroundings. Meanwhile, she proceeded further into the house, toward the bedrooms.

She found Sameer curled up on his bed, snoring. The stench of body odor and stale alcohol was overpowering. On his side of the bed, the floor was littered with at least half a dozen empty bottles. Articles of clothing were strewn every which way, on a close-by armchair, on the bed, and mingled with the bottles on the floor. The room was in darkness, and the window shutters were closed but for a few cracks that provided the only illumination. She stood over her unconscious son for minutes, watching his inert body. She was taken aback by the magnitude of the heartrending sadness that she felt for her firstborn, made worse by her powerlessness to help him. She would if she could take away all his pain and make it hers. Instead, she kissed her fingertips and brushed them on his cheek. Sameer did not stir.

The only room in the house kept pristine was her dear Faten's bedroom, undoubtedly left that way by Lubna before she went away. Evidently, her son hadn't entered the room since, because everything was exactly as she remembered. Faten's toys sat on their shelves. Her drawings hung on the wall above her desk, and her books were stacked neatly atop it. What rendered *Um Sameer* weak with emotion was the sight of the blue dress with the beaded bodice and the ruffled skirt neatly laid on the rocking chair in the corner. It was the dress that Faten should have put on for her aunt Suad's wedding, but fate, it seemed, had another idea. She walked to Faten's bed, where the covers were slightly rumpled, and she sensed it in her heart and saw it in her mind's eye, just as if it were happening right that second in front of her, the minute that Lubna sat there for the last time saying goodbye to this room and to every piece of treasure it held. She saw Lubna pick up the framed photograph of Faten with both sets of grandparents, and she saw her kiss Faten and put it back on the nightstand. She saw Lubna get up and go to Faten's certificate, which declared her the first-place winner in the short story competition. She saw Lubna touch the certificate that hung on the wall, and she saw the pride in her eyes. She saw Lubna cross the room to the door for the last time, and she saw her turn her head and glance at the dress on the rocking chair on her way, and she felt the heartbreak that her daughter-in-law felt. *Um Sameer* sat on the bed and sobbed.

She was startled out of her reverie by a crash emanating from the direction of the kitchen. *Um Sameer* lost no time; she got up and, strengthened by a new sense of purpose, rushed to her son's bedroom. Then, with one quick, clean jerk of her hand, she noisily opened the window shutters. Sameer's reaction was almost instantaneous; his head jerked in the direction of the noise, and his hands moved to his face to shield his eyes from the late afternoon sun.

"Up, up, up," she ordered. "Get up!"

Sameer groaned. His palms pressed to his eye sockets. And then he moaned again, this time louder.

"NO! Sameer," she bellowed. "I will not lose you too. Get up, out of this bed now. And out of this filth."

He lay on his back, eyes closed, hands still covering his face. Unmoving and silent.

"Get out of bed, Sameer. Let us clean this room, and you go clean yourself. And what is this filth you've been drinking? You know how your father and I feel about this kind of behavior." Her voice was stern but softer now.

"Mother, please..." he croaked hoarsely. His hands moved from his eyes to massage his temples.

"No! This is not a way to live, and I won't let you kill yourself. Up, Sameer!"

"*Meshan Allah etrikuni bhali*. Leave me be. Please!"

His anguish did nothing to deter her resolve. "I'm packing you a few things, and you will stay in Big House with us until your father and I decide what to do with you."

And with no warning, Sameer sat up on the edge of the bed, lowered his head in his hands, and began bawling like a child. Witnessing this, his mother's heart contracted in pain. She, too, would have collapsed under the same stress her son had been under. She sat next to him and took him into her arms. While he sobbed with his head resting on her bosom, she rocked him and whispered, "It'll be alright, my love, it'll be alright. Things will get better. I promise you, *habibi*."

***

While Sameer resided in Big House, and while his father shepherded him to work every morning and back every evening, and while he ate proper meals under his mother's watchful eye, he still managed to slip out of Big House most evenings and come back late at night, and sometimes not until the early morning hours. Both mother and father noticed and decided to turn a blind eye to this infraction. Both wanted him to stay under their roof for the time being and if overlooking a minor infringement of their rules would keep him there, then so be it.

During Sameer's stay at Big House, and at the end of June, while he was still wrestling with the 'call Lubna' versus 'travel to Kuwait' internal dispute, *Abu Waleed*, Lubna's father, made a fateful telephone call that sent Sameer even deeper into the abyss.

Abu Waleed had tried Sameer's house first, and after several tries with no success, tried *Abu Sameer's* house. Sameer was called to the telephone and, after a few pleasantries, had fallen silent with the receiver in his hand. *Abu Sameer* picked up the receiver from his son's hand. He held it up to his ear, another slew of pleasantries followed, and then *Abu Sameer* stilled while he listened tentatively to the other end. Finally, he replied in a clipped but civil tone and terminated the call. *Abu Sameer* put the receiver down into its cradle and looked at his son, and for the second time in six months, witnessed his son's life shatter and topple.

***

After Lubna's father made that momentous telephone call, Sameer stormed out of Big House, refusing to discuss with his parents his new predicament. He didn't return and started staying at his house again.

"Do you think he's staying here because he has no other option?" *Abu Sameer* asked his wife. "He's been indulging us, Roqaya. Let him go and figure things out for himself."

"But what if he gets into trouble?" *Um Sameer* questioned.

"What trouble? He's not a child. He's a grown man. Leave him be. What he's been through is not easy, and now Lubna wants a divorce. *Allah yueiinuh*, I pray that he makes the right decision with God's guidance." *Abu Sameer's* tone held finality in it. No more was said.

As days went by, Sameer did not show up for work and *Abu Sameer* did not question it. However, after a whole week had passed, his father decided to pay his son a visit. *Abu Sameer* recited to the bewildered and lost Sameer part of verse 229 of *Surat Al-Baqara* from the Holy Quran. "*Fa'imsak bimaruf 'aw tasrih bi'ihsan*—a woman is retained with honor and love or allowed to leave with kindness and grace."

Abu Sameer was a man who always simplified the most daunting of quandaries. In his mind, it was an open-and-shut case of two people getting married and then things not going well for them, and consequently separating. He couldn't understand why Sameer didn't understand this clear-cut situation. What man wants to be with a woman who does not want to be with him?

Yes, it was a tragedy. The death of their beloved Faten was a tragedy. The separation of her parents in its aftermath was also tragic. But Faten's death was God's will; it happened, and now everyone had to live with the aftereffects, unpleasant as they may be. Now, a week had passed since Lubna, via her father, had asked Sameer for a divorce, citing irreconcilable differences, and his son was still clinging to a clearly incompatible marriage.

To Sameer, however, it was not as open and shut a situation as his father believed. Lubna was asking for the dissolution of their marriage, but he disagreed. He wasn't ready to let her go. He knew that he could make her understand. He knew that he could win her back.

He sat in the dark, in their home, his and Lubna's. He'd been sitting this way for a while. He existed in a capsule, separated from the world. He had no idea what time of the day it was, what day of the month, or even if it was still light outside or dark. He didn't quite care anymore.

His head hurt so much. He massaged his scalp while his head rested in his hands. He wished Lubna was near him, touching him. He wanted so much to talk to her, to explain to her, to make her see. He got up and, in the dark, walked to his Faten's room. He opened the door and stood at the threshold. He had been avoiding going inside for so long because it brought back so many memories, some very painful. Or maybe he avoided Faten's bedroom because it was where Lubna stayed during her last days in this house. He should have ventured in then, talked to her, held her close to him, and explained that they would get through this and find a way together. But he didn't do that then, and it was too late now. He closed the door and retreated to the living room. He didn't want to let her go and knew he had to talk to her. He wanted to hear Lubna's voice. He must call her and must do it now. She doesn't want this. A divorce couldn't be her idea, he was sure of it.

On the third ring, the call was answered. He heard *Um*

Waleed's voice say, "Hello…"

Silence.

She repeated, "Hello?" and then, "Who is this?"

He said nothing. His head hurt so much. He wanted to put the receiver down but didn't.

A long silence followed, and just when he thought *Um Waleed* was about to end the call, he heard her muffled voice say, "Lubna, *habibti*, I think it's for you."

Seconds elapsed, during which Sameer heard low, unintelligible voices, and then he felt Lubna's presence on the other end of the line even before he heard her voice. Her soft breathing was followed by an even softer "Yes."

So many words were fighting to get out, so many things he wanted to say and explain, so many of his actions he needed to rationalize. Nevertheless, as usually was the case, his words betrayed him. "Lubna, I…" And then he fell silent. "I…"

"No," she said. "No," she said again, this time with more resolve. She had anticipated what he was thinking. She knew him, after all. "I know what you are thinking, and I know what I want." Her words were clear and concise.

"But I need to tell you something," he said.

"Sameer, please. Just let me go." Her tone was still soft but unquestionably confident.

"But I love you," he said in anguish.

There followed a silence, after which Lubna said the last words he would ever hear her say: "I know you do, so for me, please release me."

As excruciating as her request was to hear, be that as it may, he understood it perfectly.

***

Abu Sameer decided that he and Sameer were to leave on their annual European shopping trip for textiles and fabrics in the middle of July. The rescheduled date was earlier than he would have preferred, but the current circumstances necessitated extraordinary measures. Sameer was disinclined to agree, but he didn't have the fight in him to oppose his father, so the plan was set.

On the eve of their travel, *Abu Sameer* made a suggestion to his wife: "Why don't you and the girls give Sameer's house a visit while he's away?"

"I was planning to do just that," she said.

"Try to remove any unpleasant reminders," he said and then added conspiratorially, "if you can."

This statement, *Um Sameer* decided, would better be assessed and interpreted on-site and only after she saw the state of her son's house, not before.

***

Um Sameer let herself into Sameer's house. Four of her daughters accompanied her on this visit, including the twins, the newlywed Suad, and Asma. The last of the four attended only after voicing her reluctance to join their escapade, adding that, firstly, she was no one's maid, and secondly, she felt it was none of their business to dispose of Lubna's belongings. To which her mother had replied, "Keep quiet, keep your opinions to yourself, and follow me inside."

The interior was not as miserable as on her last visit. The place had an unaired smell, but everything seemed to be in its proper place. No empty bottles or dirty clothes strewn around. Except for a few dirty dishes and glasses in the sink, the kitchen was as the twins had left it on their last visit.

Um Sameer opened all the windows and shutters, allowing bright sunlight to fill the rooms. The first thing everyone noticed simultaneously was the absence of Sameer and Lubna's wedding photo that used to hang on the living room wall. Registering this, all heads turned in unison to look at the bare surface of the dining room's sideboard, where a framed photograph of Lubna once stood.

Room by room they went, and little by little they discovered that every trace of Lubna had vanished. Finally, in the main bedroom, *Um Sameer* noticed that Lubna's side of the closet, her vanity, and dresser were devoid of any article that ever belonged to her. Not a comb or a tube of lipstick remained.

When did this happen? How did Sameer manage it? And what did he do with Lubna's belongings? No one knew precisely. He hadn't discussed it with anyone in his family, nor had he asked for their help.

"Well, as long as we're here, let's not just stand around twiddling our thumbs," *Um Sameer* announced to her daughters and followed the announcement with a specific order for each daughter.

Once her daughters were otherwise occupied, she entered Faten's bedroom and closed the door behind her. She felt the familiar constriction of grief in her heart and throat as she gazed at Faten's toys, books, and a photo of her with her four grandparents.

The occupants of Big House seldom took photographs. The few pictures hanging on the walls were two still-life drawings that adorned the living room, and an image of the Dome of the Rock *Qubbat al-Sakhrah* graced the guest room. Photos were rare and usually kept in photo albums tucked away in closets. In Sameer and Lubna's home, however, framing and displaying pictures was a big thing, no doubt one of Lubna's influences. *Um Sameer* realized that now, with Lubna's photos disappearing, it didn't feel right that she only had a miniature wedding photo of her son and his bride, several of Sameer alone, one or two of Faten, but curiously, not one of them together. They were a family, after all, a beautiful family, a family she loved regardless of recent developments and the divorce. She wanted to remember them as they once were. *Um Sameer* knew exactly what she was looking for and where to find it. About a year ago, Faten shared a delightful secret about her bedside photo frame with her grandmother. She explained how she enjoyed switching between two pictures every week because she treasured both of them equally.

Um Sameer picked up the framed photograph of Faten with both sets of grandparents and turned the frame to its backside. She removed the back cover and then took out its contents: a blank cardboard card, and another picture hidden between the displayed photo and the cardboard card. The photograph featured Sameer in a dark suit and Lubna in a dark skirt with a sleeveless white shirt. Lubna was smiling, but her gaze was directed toward Faten sitting between them. Faten, around six or seven, wore a white dress with puffy sleeves, and her hair was tied into a ponytail with a white ribbon bow.

Part 2

NUHA'S STORY

CHAPTER 4

1

My father had another family before he married my mother and had me. Tragedy befell his first family, which paved the way for my life to begin thirteen years later.

During my childhood and as far back as my memories take me, and during our frequent visits to Big House, there wasn't much talk about the first family. I was able to catch a few words thrown around and some whispers here and there, all out of earshot of my father, who, it seemed, had declared the whole subject taboo. Big House didn't have any framed photos of them displayed on walls, shelves, or even tucked away in old photo albums. The only photo of my father's first family that I did manage to find was in one of my grandmother's boxes filled with piles of knickknacks and old photographs. A small black and white photo of my much younger father in a dark suit, seated beside a smart-looking woman in a dark skirt and a sleeveless white shirt, with dark wavy shoulder-length hair parted in the middle and smiling but not looking into the camera. Instead, she was looking at the young girl sitting between her and my father. The little girl was about my age when I found the photo, around six or seven. She wore a white dress with puffy sleeves; she was pretty with a small nose and large eyes and hair tied into a ponytail with a white ribbon bow. By the time I found that photo, I knew who the woman and the girl were and what they epitomized. But it had taken me some time to piece together this information.

I was about five when I first heard the name Faten. I caught one of my aunts looking at me and then saying, "Faten was prettier." To which a younger aunt replied, "But they look so much alike! Don't they?!" I had yet to learn who this Faten was and what the name represented. No one had ever mentioned to me an older sister, now deceased. I'm sure that my mother would have told me eventually, but maybe she was waiting for the right time to explain the sibling I would never get to meet. However, the aunts were not as patient as my mother, and it seemed they were itching for me to dig into the past and inquire. Hence, the glib comments and the sly hints, and so forth.

I believe my aunts were incredulous at my lack of curiosity. They were mistaken, of course; all children have an innate inquisitive nature. My explanations for not satisfying my aunts' desires are threefold. Primarily, although I fail to understand the reasons now, back then, I had this inexplicable fear of the aunts, so even if I'd wanted to probe, this apprehension prevented me.

Secondly, my time as a child was preoccupied mainly with reading. My mother told me I was about four when I walked up to her and asked her what was in her hand and what she was doing with it. At the time, she was reading a book. She explained. I told her I wanted to do the same. The very next day, she started teaching me the alphabet. By the time I started first grade, I had made another new discovery: in addition to the Arabic alphabet, there was another alphabet, the English one. It was during the summer break following first grade that I first heard the word 'bookworm' used to describe me. While other little girls my age were outside playing hopscotch or inside dressing and undressing dolls, I was in my room with my head in a storybook. On occasions when we visited Big House, I always had a book in my hand, and I would sit next to Grandma Roqaya on the portico and read to her and show her all the pictures. My grandmother never learned to read herself; nonetheless, she had an immense love for books, and cherished all my grandfather's books and manuscripts, dusted them, or supervised others to do just that, and took great care of them and never let anyone touch them but for a privileged few. Thus, to my aunts' displeasure, it was clear that I had no time to be drawn into their web of games and pursuits, which vexed them immeasurably. All their hints of Faten did this or that, or Faten was prettier, cleverer, smarter, and so on, went unanswered but certainly not unnoticed.

Finally, there was another reason my aunts' endeavors went unsatisfied. Three months into first grade, a second-grader named Lina told me what she'd heard through the grapevine. Her mother had some friends over, and they got talking, and Lina heard it all. Lina's storytelling abilities and spinning of the perfect tale were exceptional for a girl so young. She twisted and swayed, made quite a theatrical performance that day, and delivered a compelling narrative that left me curious and skeptical.

"You are such a liar!!" I remember shouting.

To which she answered in her indignant default setting, "What!? Lying is forbidden. It's *haram*! I'm not lying, Nuha."

But even while accusing her of deceit, my mind was working in overdrive and inserting the scattered pieces of information I had collected over the years into proper order.

This was when I did the most sensible thing a little girl does in such circumstances: I went to my mother. I told her what Lina said and asked, "Who is Faten? And is it true that she died?"

My mother told me the whole story. When I asked her why she hadn't told me before, she said, "Because I didn't want my baby to be unhappy." She also said that what had happened all those years ago made my father very sad, and although he loved us very much and loved me most especially, it's better not to talk to him about Faten *Allah yerhamha* because that will only make him sadder.

2

At the time of my conception, my mother was surprised to be having a baby at her age. My father, seven years her senior, was fifty-four by the time I came into this world. Not a great age by any means to be starting a new family. He was not as thrilled as many would have expected, and to make things worse, my birth fell but two days short of the anniversary of the tragedy that had transpired years earlier.

His presence in our time together as father and daughter was inconsequential until the last few years of his life. He was always there and behind the scenes, but played a minor role in my upbringing. Financially, my father was solid and dependable, but that's where his responsibility of raising a daughter ended and where he chose to hand the duty over to others. He was always present throughout my school and college years. Still, he rarely showed any interest in either the curricular or the extracurricular of my activities. I saw him almost daily at mealtimes and in the evenings, but he did little and said even less.

The way I justified my father's behavior in my young mind was with the thought that he was too heartbroken the first time; he didn't want to repeat the experience a second time around. Maybe it was because he never wanted to grow too attached, or at least that is what I chose to believe. I still, to this day, try desperately to find excuses for his detachment. Justifications are readily available in my mind, more for my benefit than for anyone else's. Yet, now, years after his passing, my memories of him are not unpleasant. He was a rock; he was dependable and steady, never capricious with his emotions. He was what he was, and he never wavered from it. Our relationship, although reserved, was solid until the end.

3

Big House (*El-beit El-kbeer*) is not big. In fact, it's quite small. Located in an old part of Amman, now turned into a fashionable area and a cultural tourist magnet, it was built in the 1920s. The house is a simple rectangular structure with a semi-circular entrance portico and is surrounded on all four sides by spruce trees. With a limestone facade and ornamented tile floors, the property has had many purchase offers in recent years. But, contrary to her neighbors, who capitulated and sold for very handsome profits, my grandmother refused to even consider selling her home.

I honestly don't know why we call it Big House. All children, grandchildren, and great-grandchildren refer to it by that name, and for as long as I can recall, that name has been synonymous with family, big gatherings, loud noise, and good food.

During their marriage, my paternal grandparents produced nine offspring. Grandmother Roqaya was eighteen when she gave birth to her firstborn, Sameer. Sameer, my father, was named after his own grandfather. Unfortunately, however, Sameer senior had died six months before the birth of his namesake, which somewhat dampened the festivity.

My grandparents went on to produce another eight children, all girls. Sameera, Muneera, Asma, Mona, Laila, and Suad. At the time of my aunt Suad's birth, my grandmother had almost abandoned the hope of ever producing a brother for Sameer. She told anyone interested that she was happy with what *Allah* had given her, *Alhamdulillah* praise be to God. Yet, seven years later, when my grandmother was forty, my grandparents made one last attempt, and that was when my twin aunts Feryal and Fatima came into the world.

4

My paternal grandmother was a fierce old lady, considered by many as a tyrant and a menace. To those who truly understood her, she was tough but with hidden softness invisible to most. Everyone respected her, some loved her, and only a few knew how to appease her. Of her nine children, only four fell into that last category. And of her grandchildren, only I found the doorway to the workings of her intellect.

Except for a hunched back and frailness of the body, which inevitably accompanies old age, neither her internal organs nor her mind failed her up to her last breath. Then, suddenly, they just stopped working one evening in her sleep at the ripe old age of a hundred and five. That night, she went to bed determined to make the housekeeper clean all the windows early the following morning, and she did not wake up. This took place during my 'bad period,' the second year of that time to be precise. During that chapter of my life, my parents decided to move back to Big House and take care of me there. They knew my attachment to my grandmother and hoped it would help, and maybe it did help a little.

Saturday 13 August

My name is Faten and I am 8 years old.

My mommy gave me this notebook for my birthday.

My mommy said that it is called a diary, like she
had when she was small like me. I will start 3 grade
after 3 weeks. My mommy said that if I write
every day in this note book (diary) my english will
be better like my arabic. She siad I can ask her how
to write a word and she will help if I want.

Every day I will write the best thing that happens
to me in that day.

Mommy said it will be a secret. I think she is
saying the truth. I can hide it if I want to because
I dont want any one to read it. I don't want M to
read it.

Today was my birthday. We had a big cake and
presents. Grand dad got me a doll house. I promise
that I will not play alot with it when school starts.

My grand mom got me a green sweeter (yuk).
Daddy got me 5 books and siad if I read alot I will
write better. Mommy got me a gold earing and
this not book (diary).   42
Mommy siad when I go to school she will take a
cake to class for my friends. I dont want that but
I dont tell her that.

Tomorrow I will write again.

Good night now.

CHAPTER 5

1

I am tired, and my head and eyes ache from staring too long at my computer screen. I wish more than ever not to see the loathsome red car parked in the street. I need a break. He's been coming more often than usual recently. I need to find Khaled alone and talk to him on the subject. I need to tell him how I feel. And I need him to know that I'm on his side and that I understand.

I turn left and round the bend, and there it is, the red Prius, parked in front of our building. I park on the other side of the road. As if parking in front of it or behind it will tarnish me in some way. I take a deep breath and then another. His bitterness fuels some hateful emotion deep inside me, but I don't want to meditate on this right now. I hear my heart hammer in my throat and feel my nails dig into my palms as I make the walk from the car to my door. I turn the key.

2

He, the object of my loathing, is doing something mundane cross-legged on the apartment floor. He is tampering with our electric fan and causing quite the racket. Clearly, he doesn't know what he is doing but acts like he does. It is his way of blowing off steam and venting his frustration, which I know because it is a performance I have witnessed on other furniture and appliances in the apartment. His body language shows he registers my presence. Still, he doesn't acknowledge me or look up, but I hear him mutter and curse incoherently.

In my mind, I am enjoying a recurring fantasy; my knee colliding with this guy's balls and him twisting on the floor in agony, which alarmingly brings me immense pleasure. Lately—and by that, I mean the last year or so—images of inflicting bodily harm on this man have increased in intensity and frequency. Reality, however, is a different story. I paint a smile and clear my throat, forcing him to look up. Playing nice is not a trait I excel at, but I'll do anything for Khaled. So, I try to appease the guy on my floor by nodding and agreeing with whatever he's prattling on about.

3

I sit on the living room sofa, massaging my aching feet. He discarded the electric fan and went inside to Khaled's bedroom. I hear muffled voices, and a heated argument ensues. This takes five minutes, then silence for another ten or so minutes. A door opens and slams. He walks to the apartment's door and leaves without a word, ignoring me altogether. Still, curiously enough and indeed out of character, he shuts the door softly behind him.

I get up and make for Khaled's room. But instead, I see him leaning on the doorjamb that connects the living room to the bedrooms. His face is stoic; I know that look so well, the look of the resigned. I don't like it.

No preamble, I say, "This is not a phase, and it won't pass. You do know that, right?"

He looks straight ahead and sighs, not meeting my eyes. I hate when he does that. I know him so well, inside and out. He's my best friend, my person, the one who made me (almost) whole again.

"It doesn't matter…" he says.

"It does matter! It will always matter, Khaled. You matter.

I hate seeing you like this."

He looks me in the eyes now and says quietly, "When I look into the mirror, I recognize the person that looks back at me. I still like what I see, so leave it, Nuha."

Always with a flair for the dramatic, my Khaled. I can't help but smile when he comes back with such declarations.

"Big words," I say playfully.

He chuckles. "Maybe there was some exaggeration there for effect, but honestly, Nuha, it's all good. Please believe me. I will fix this," he replies.

With that, he leans in, brushes a kiss on my cheek, and leaves me standing there staring at his retreating back. I don't know what else to say, so I say nothing.

4

I'm a creature of habit. I wasn't always one, but my days have been running at a cyclic pace in recent years. Dinner in my pajamas and movie time is drawing close, and Khaled has not reappeared. I pass several times back and forth close to his closed door. Shuffle my feet and try to make some noise to no avail. I knock gently, and there is no answer. I decide on a different tactic, luring him out using my culinary talents. I make my famous scrambled eggs and leave the kitchen door ajar; maybe he'll catch a whiff and come running. I hear movement; it's working. I listen as his bedroom door opens and busy myself nonchalantly washing the frying pan. He walks into the kitchen and doesn't say a word, just picks up two pieces of white toast and puts them in the toaster.

"You know, you should learn to make something other than eggs, wife." His voice is playful, and some dark cloud that I didn't know was over my head lifts.

"You're just jealous I'm a better cook, husband." I grin and wink. "I just needed something quick and smelly to lure you out."

"As for you being the better cook, you wish!" Khaled says just before shoveling a generous forkful of scrambled eggs into his mouth.

I look at him in wonder and delight as he finishes and almost licks the plate clean. "You still love me, yes?" I ask.

"I adore you! You know that. But I don't want to talk about it, Nuha," he replies.

"Ok. I don't, either. Not now, but..."

"But... when I want to talk, you're there for me. I know, *habibti*. I know." He walks over to the sink where I'm standing and hugs me.

What I want to say but don't: I wish you could see what I see when you are with him. Instead, I say, "What's tonight's movie?"

He recites three names, and we end up watching *Catch and Release* for the umpteenth time.

"When are we going to Boulder, Colorado?" I ask.

"Soon," he replies.

5

I look in the mirror. Do I like the person looking back at me? Do I recognize her? A few years ago, both questions would have been redundant because I rarely looked in a mirror, except when I glanced at my reflection while using the bathroom for other purposes. Back then, I recognized myself well enough. I knew the worthless person leering back at me. Taunting me, making fun of me.

My father once saw me looking in a mirror in Big House. *Baba*, who, for as long as I can remember, raised me by relinquishing the task to my mother and grandmother and observing from afar, took a different stance during my 'bad period.' We became kindred spirits, he and I. He approached me while I was gazing in that sitting room mirror; I must have been standing there for a long time. I remember him taking me into his arms, holding me, and rocking me. *Baba* was tall; he rested his chin on my head and held me for a long time. I remember the dampness in my hair and on my scalp. I knew he was crying. Maybe he was crying for me. Maybe he was crying for himself. Maybe for both. It didn't matter why he was crying. The important thing is that my *Baba*, of all people, knew precisely how it felt.

Now I look in the mirror. I look at my scrubbed face. At my wet hair. Do I like this person?

After the movie tonight, we went out to the balcony—no stars in the sky, just blackness.

"When are we going to *Wadi Rum**?" I asked.

"Soon," Khaled replied.

Silence for a few minutes, and then he said, "When was the last time I told you that you're the best thing that's ever happened to me?"

"Not for a while," I answered.

"You are," he said.

Every time he says it, I believe it more. I'm starting to like what I see in the mirror—a little more every day.

---

* Wadi Rum: Valley cut in sandstone and granite rock in southern Jordan. Named UNESCO World Heritage site in 2011.

Sunday 21 August

The best thing that happened to me today is that daddy got a dog. Daddy said that this is the real birthday present and not the books. He siad that the books are also important.

It is a great dog and it is a boy dog. Daddy siad we can give it a name and I siad I want it to be Tiger.

Mommy laughed and siad a Tiger is a cat and daddy siad it is a funny name for a dog. I think it is a great name for a dog.

M siad it is a stupid name. I think he is stupid.

M siad he want the name Caesar.

Daddy siad that Tiger + Caesar = Taesar

Our dog is called Taesar!

Mummy thinks it is a briliant name.

I found M in my room today. I think that he wants to find this diary. But he didnt I'm the best hider in the world.

Good night ☺

CHAPTER 6

1

Khaled and I meet at noon. It is our weekly pilgrimage to Big House. Every Tuesday, like clockwork, we visit my mother and the Young Aunts and have lunch. Naturally, my mother expects it, and the Young Aunts need their weekly dose of taunting Khaled and me, something we have come to expect and surreptitiously enjoy. The topics thrown at us range from trivial things—like hair too long, somewhat short, much too dark, blouse too dull, body too thin or too chubby—to more significant issues, like why Khaled, an engineer, works as a personal trainer instead of engineering. And the all-time favorite subject, babies, or the lack thereof, and that we're not getting any younger!

The repartee between Khaled and my aunts is entertaining to the point that I find my mother chuckling in anticipation before the exchange starts. This, in and of itself, is a joy to me because I love to see her happy. In the beginning, I was afraid Khaled might be offended, but I needn't have worried. I soon realized Khaled dished out as well as he received, and the aunts thought he was hilarious. He has this incredible ability to conciliate people and situations, and soon after, I started to feel the warmth in their banter.

2

Feryal and Fatima are in their seventies. All the family refers to them as *El-ammat Es-sghar*, the Young Aunts. Both are spinsters, although Fatima never tires of telling everyone about her betrothed, whom she dumped two weeks before the big day. Maybe apart from her twin, nobody alive today knows why this happened, and she never offers an explanation. The fact that the jilted fiancée married someone else six months after the incident never dampens her excitement in recounting the story.

My mother stayed in Big House after my father passed away, and I moved out. I secretly appreciate that she's not alone and has company; the three make up a merry bunch. Outwardly, they squabble and argue all day long. Inwardly, however, I recognize the affection they have for one another.

3

We reach the portico and listen; the noise emanating from the inside suggests that today is different. The occupants of the house have company. My mother's steps are slow, and she takes her time to make it to the door, which gives us ample time to hear the loud and echoing laughter coming from the living room. I brace myself for a colorful afternoon.

"Suad and Luna are here," my mother says, kissing my cheek. "They are staying for lunch," she adds with a kiss to Khaled's cheek. "I made stuffed chicken." With her back to us, she ambles to the kitchen.

"Why didn't you call and tell me, Mama?" I ask, following in her footsteps.

"I thought you liked Luna and Suad," she counters, and then adds with the slightest roll of the eyes, "and Khokha."

"No, Mama, of course I love them. I just don't like surprises... Forget it, *habibti*, how are you?"

"They're too loud. You know how I feel about loud voices..." Mama says, shaking her head sorrowfully.

That's not true, of course. My mother may appear a reserved person on first impression, but she's as loud as they come among family and acquaintances.

I glance at Khaled and see him standing over the stove, busy opening pots and gazing into pans. Sampling with his fingers and then double-dipping. A habit I'm still working to abolish.

"They didn't call or even text; they just showed up. Luckily, I made enough food," Mama adds in a hushed voice.

I smile inwardly at the word 'text.' A firm opposer in the not-too-distant past to the smartphone, my mother refused to own one. Claiming she didn't need it and couldn't begin to understand how to use it. Nowadays, however, texting, or the more convenient voice messaging, has become her favorite mode of communication.

Khokha barges into the kitchen, followed by a harassed-looking Luna, trailed by an equally harassed-looking Gigi, the Filipino housekeeper. Before Luna registers my presence, Khokha reverses tactics and runs back out, and she retreats. Gigi makes a beeline to the stove, slaps Khaled's hands, closes the pots, and shoos him out of the kitchen. Khaled obliges and runs out after Khokha, shouting, "Where's my favorite person in the world?!"

4

I enter the sitting room. The Young Aunts are on either side of the sofa, and Aunt Suad is on the armchair beside them. Heads together, whispering conspiratorially and ignoring me and everyone else.

Luna, Suad's youngest granddaughter, sits on the other armchair, panting from the earlier exertion, and watches her five-year-old son. The two Khaleds are on the floor. The older Khaled tickles the younger one, better known as Khokha, and the latter squeals in delight.

Feryal's loud burst mars this picture of domestic bliss. "What an idiot!!" she bellows. All fall silent—even the tickling stops.

"What are you smiling at?" she snaps at Khaled.

"Just admiring your beauty," Khaled replies.

Feryal scoffs and goes back to the business of ignoring everyone but the other two sisters. It is not difficult to discern who the 'idiot' in question is. For years now, there has been a war waging with periods of remission and other periods of exacerbation between these three sisters and their other sister, Asma, who is still alive and living in Amman.

I can never keep up with the intricate branching of our family tree. Therefore, I'm always grateful for Aunt Fatima, who has a mind that revels in chronicling every birth, death, marriage, and divorce in the family. When needed, she is the authority one goes to for names and dates. Aunt Sameera and Aunt Muneera, *Allah yerhamhom*, passed away in 1984 and 2002, respectively. They left behind a brood, all married now with children and grandchildren of their own. My memories of the eldest two aunts are patchy; they were married and living in Saudi Arabia with their families since long before I was born. On occasions when they visited Big House, and I happened to be there, I remember a lot of bickering between them and my grandmother.

Aunts Mona and Laila married brothers and soon after immigrated to the United States. I only saw Aunt Mona once when I was about eight or nine. Then when I was sixteen, we got the news that she had died after battling breast cancer. Aunt Laila came to Amman a few years ago when Grandmother passed away. When I saw her frail frame, I wondered how she could have made the long flight from the States and how she would survive the journey back. She was accompanied by her daughter Salam and Salam's daughter Melanie. Still, at the time, I was battling my own demons, and I didn't venture to get to know any of them. They've never been back since, nor do I expect to see them anytime in the foreseeable future.

However, like all twenty-first-century families, we are connected via social media nowadays. Of course, we don't really know each other, but we all keep track, like, react, and comment on each other's photos, birthdays, engagements, weddings, deaths, illnesses, trips, coffee with friends, fresh cakes out of the oven, and so much more.

5

My grandmother's penultimate pregnancy resulted in my Aunt Suad. She and the Young Aunts are as thick as thieves. Suad has an imposing character, and although they would be loath to admit it, the Young Aunts are afraid of her. In addition to my father, her firstborn and only son, the three youngest of her daughters had the strongest connection with their mother, which ultimately impacted my relationship with them. Of all the aunts, my relationship is strongest with the youngest three. They were present during my childhood and my teens, and I encountered them the most at Big House.

This brings me to the 'idiot' in question, my Aunt Asma. An old lady in her eighth decade. She lives not too far from Big House. Although we are not too close, I admire her nerve and tenacity. Until three years ago, Aunt Asma had her own car and drove herself around to her social engagements. Then, after a mild fender bender and because of her advancing years, her sons insisted on hiring a chauffeur to transport her around the city. Married to a well-to-do merchant, now deceased, her social circles are somewhat different than those of her sisters, a fact of which she never grows weary of reminding them. Considers herself the social bunny; she roams from brunch in so-and-so cafe to lunch with friends to other similar activities. But this is not why she's labeled an 'idiot' by her younger sisters.

Aunt Asma has five children, all sons, and all lawyers. Her crime is that her sons are the principal advocates for selling Big House and distributing the proceeds to all legal heirs. A heinous offense that the younger sisters take very seriously.

Since my grandfather died, my grandmother refused to sell under the pretense, "*Allah* willing, I only have a few more years. You can't wait?!!" Or something to the effect of, "You want to throw me into the streets!? Is that what you want?"

Of course, that would not have been the case. Had they sold the property, her cut alone would have bought her a very handsome apartment in a good neighborhood. Yet my grandmother was not someone to argue with, and she was right—it was her home, and she was an old woman, after all. However, my grandmother outlived her husband by twenty-seven years. Three of her daughters passed away before her, and her only son and firstborn, my father, died only two years after her.

6

My mother announces, "Lunch is ready, *tafadalu*, enjoy."

We all move to the north-facing balcony, where the table is set for the occasion. Once upon a time, this balcony was the family room in the summer months, turned into children's sleeping area on warm nights. However, now that the occupants' number has dwindled to only four, the balcony is mostly the dining room, weather permitting.

"Thank you, *hayati*, my dear; looks and smells delicious," Khaled says, digging in even before the rest are in their seats.

"You shouldn't have, Auntie Sarah!" Luna comments. "Everything looks so beautiful."

"Oh, it was nothing, *habibti*," my mother replies. "Enjoy! Do you want Gigi to take Khokha off your hands for a while?"

Gigi enters the balcony carrying a bowl of something; I notice her shooting daggers at my mother. She sets the bowl down and flees.

"Khokha will sit here right next to me, won't you, *habibi*?" I say to the kid clutching his mom's leg.

"No!" he replies—his favorite word.

"Gigiii!" my mother cries out.

"Leave her alone, Sarah," Feryal interjects. "She hasn't had a minute all morning. Cooking and running after Khokha, and I don't know what... *Allah Yueiinaha*, God help her!"

Mama looks indignant, but it is true. My mother is growing weaker every day. A fact I don't like to ponder much; her household duties these days consist of her sitting in the kitchen barking orders at Gigi. And Gigi, God bless her, does everything my mother and the Young Aunts ask, and says extraordinarily little.

Gigi, short for Georgina, hails from the Philippines. She came to Amman about fifteen years ago. She claims to be an orphan with no family back in her hometown. However, since she set foot in Big House, she has yet to go home to visit and saves all her wages. An excellent cook—credits to my grandmother—and an exceptional housekeeper. Gigi was around when my grandmother died, and she helped my mother and me take care of my father during his last few months. I consider her a godsend and a pillar of Big House. Her presence takes a lot of pressure off my shoulders regarding my mother and aunts.

7

Khaled, Luna, and I sit around the dining table after lunch.

"He's flying to Dubai for two days, and then we're thinking of going to Turkey for a week or so, maybe Marmaris," Luna tells me about her husband and their plans for the summer.

Khaled's phone vibrates, and he looks at the screen. When two people are in sync, one knows by the slightest gesture of the other that something is amiss. He picks up his phone and moves to the railing. He talks for a few seconds and ends the call. Comes back to the table and sits down. To anyone else, nothing has changed; he just took a call. To me, however, he is a transformed person, and I know instinctively who caused this transformation.

"We want somewhere for Khokha to enjoy, with a swimming pool, kids' activities..." Luna continues talking, and I'm trying to keep up, but I can't; my concentration fizzles.

Back in the sitting room, the three sisters decide over three cups of steaming mint tea that their sister Asma committed some malicious act, and she must be punished. We hear loud voices and expletives, and the television is blasting at maximum volume now, which adds to the cacophony. What her crime is precisely and what the penance will be is anyone's guess. Nothing will come of it, just a few angry and bored old ladies letting out steam because they can do little else.

8

We say our goodbyes with perfunctory cheek-kissing. Promises to see you next week. Keep safe. Remember your medication. Call me if you want anything, anytime.

I glance at Gigi, who satisfies me with a bob of her head. Wordlessly communicating, 'Don't worry, all is good. I'll take care of them.'

Luna sees us at the door. We promise to see each other soon for coffee. A promise we both know we will break, but we lovingly hug regardless.

I know the answer before I ask the question, but I ask it anyway on the walk to our cars. "What movie are we watching tonight?" I try to sound relaxed. I put my hand into Khaled's and squeeze it tightly.

He squeezes back, and we keep walking. When we get to my car, Khaled says, "*Habibti*, I'm not going home with you now. I might be late. Don't wait for me. Ok?"

I say nothing and look down at the asphalt in the road when he says, "Nuha, I'm trying to fix things. Please understand. I need to do this."

I hug him. "When was the last time I told you that you're the second-best thing that's ever happened to me?" I ask with a laugh, trying to lighten the mood.

"Not for a while," he replies.

"You are," I say.

He hugs me back tight.

9

I step into my home, my sanctuary, my favorite place in the world at this junction of my life.

I do not want to think about anything. So instead, I go about my nighttime routine methodically and in quick succession.

I turn my bedside lamp on and turn off the main light switch. I sit on my bed. I look at my nightstand. On it are two framed photographs and two spiral notebooks. One of the spiral notebooks is solid blue, and the other has a dandelion on the cover. I pick up one frame and kiss the picture it holds. I pick up the other frame and do the same. I get under the covers and pick up the notebook with the dandelion. I read one page, close it, and return it to where I found it. I do not pick up the other notebook, not today.

I switch off the light.

I wait for sleep to come.

Tonight, it looks like sleep will elude me.

Monday 29 august

Mommy took us today to buy school things because school is next week.

I dont like school but I dont tell mommy. I like school but not the girls in my school. I dont like the boys too. I think they are all stupid.

I dont like the teachers. Some times they are meen to me.

The best thing that happened to me today is that mommy made chocolat cake.

I wish school is not next week.

Good night.

CHAPTER 7

1

"This is a bookshop with coffee. Not a coffee shop with books!" I have heard Tea exclaim on several occasions, sometimes adding under her breath, "You illiterate fools!"

My friend and partner, Tahani, referred to by her employees and everyone else—save me—as Madam T, is an eccentric woman with a capital E. The first time I heard her being called Madam T, I remember mentally writing it in Arabic and then in English in quick succession. Maybe I was thirsty then or cold and needed something to warm me up, but since that day, she is simply Tea, the beverage.

The place I first happened to meet Tea is called 'The Place'. I stumbled upon it a few years back while on one of my aimless roamings around town. It was an autumn afternoon when I took that fateful walk not too far from Big House. The Place is on a lane off the main street. I remember the traffic was terrible that day, making me take the first turn to get away from the din. A few steps ahead, two notices side by side in The Place's window caught my eye: "90% Off!!" said one of them, and "Clearance Sale! All (My Babies) Must Go!" said the other. Reclaimed wood framed the glass storefront holding the two announcements. The same wood also made the door to the right of the facade. On either side from the inside, lush curtains encased the window, complete with potted plants on the sill, giving the appearance that I was looking into someone's living room.

I was fascinated with the overall rustic appearance of The Place, and I may have stood there staring in for longer than was natural for an ordinary person because I remember this lady coming out of the door and asking me if I was alright. She was a person of considerable size; on that day, she was dressed in a knee-length navy blue wraparound dress with pink bows on the shoulders and mint-colored sandals. Her white hair with light orange streaks was cut short and stood out every which way. I recall the colors quite clearly because I remember thinking that she reminded me of a multicolored box of macarons.

"Are you alright, *habibti?*" she asked, and when I didn't answer and just looked at her blankly, she said, "Come in; you look cold, and you're blue." And she walked back in, holding the door open for me to follow; I did.

"By blue, I don't mean sad. I mean freezing!" she said, leading me to sit on the leather sofa in the middle of the shop. "Not that you look ecstatically happy, mind you..." she prattled on.

I sat down as instructed and looked around; the interior was as warm and inviting as its exterior. The Place was a bookshop, and wood, not unlike the kind I saw outside, made up the floor-to-ceiling bookshelves and the hardwood floors. The woody colors and textures supplied a warm and comfortable ambiance; oddly, it gave me a feeling of sitting in Big House, a sense of home.

I rested on a Chesterfield leather two-seater situated in the center of the room. The colorful lady sat opposite me on one of the two high-backed leather armchairs. Between us stood a no-nonsense solid wood coffee table with no frill or flounce. While my sofa was faded brown, her chair was a deep red leather. Underfoot was a Tabriz Persian rug, not unlike the ones in Big House, although smaller. The whole effect added to that feeling of well-being still growing inside me.

My eyes roamed around, taking everything in; an antique-looking oak desk decorated the left side of the store, nestled between the bookshelves. I still needed to figure out how I could have missed this place before today. As if it was con-jured up from thin air, nothing at all, and then there it was, right in my way, blocking my path and forcing me to stand still and notice it.

I nevertheless had to open my mouth and say something to this woman, but I had nothing to say. At that time in my life, and during my walks, I rarely encountered situations where I had to talk to people. In fact, I had actively avoided crowds and people in general. I walked then because I needed to get out of the house and escape from my parents' constant attention. They were suffocating me, trying their damned-est to do anything for me. I felt sorry for them, much sorrier than I had felt for myself, and that was precisely why I had to escape them. I wandered without an aim or goal in sight, except to grow weary so that when I got back home, I would fall into a dreamless slumber.

On that pivotal day, I met the person who would remove me from my rut, giving me a reason to start to find a purpose to get up every morning. Was it her charisma, appearance, or energy? I didn't know exactly. Or maybe it was me; I had decided the time had come to do just that. I had contemplated ending it all on many occasions; especially at the beginning, I had thought seriously about ending my futile existence. And I might have succeeded had it not been for some primal instinct that prevented me and kept me holding on. This same instinct pushed me that day to The Place, to that store, to sit in front of that nice, bubbly person and look around me and think to myself, 'Coffee might bring in more customers.'

"This place needs coffee," I said matter-of-factly.

"Sajaaaa!" the colorful lady screamed at the top of her lungs.

An agitated-looking young lady poked her head from the door marked 'Private, Employees Only' at the far back of the shop a few seconds later, saying, "Yep, what is it, Madam T?"

"Is there any coffee left back there? Or did I drink it all?" she cackled.

"Nope, all finished, and I washed the pot. Plus, I'm still on the last task you assigned me, and I only have two hands. Can I go now?" Obviously, a girl with a short fuse.

Madam T, whom I will refer to as Tea from here onwards, said to the girl who had already disappeared through the door and out of sight, "Go, go! Sorry I asked."

To me she said, "I'll go make a fresh pot. Meanwhile, why don't you look around," gesturing to the books strewn everywhere. Hardcovers and paperbacks of every size, shape, and creed lined every shelf and flat surface. Piled on the coffee table, on the far table at the back, on a table at the front near the entrance, on the antique desk, stacked on the floor, and books still in their boxes. Just then, I registered that The Place was about to burst at the seams from too many books.

"But that's not what I mean," I said. "The coffee is for The Place to jumpstart it. I, personally, prefer tea!"

2

"But this is a bookshop, not a coffee shop!!" Tea said.

"And you are shutting it down," I explained. "Because apparently, not many people are coming in to browse and buy your 'babies,' or am I mistaken?"

She appraised me up and down, but said nothing. So, I continued, "You have a '90% off' sign in your window, and you still have no one in here!"

Still no comment from Tea, and I took that as an encouragement to go on. "You need to kick-start this place. We must invite people in and find ways to keep them in."

"For someone who hasn't said a thing for an hour, you sure have a lot to say!" she chuckled.

Looking back on that day, both Tea and I simultaneously noticed the change of the pronoun 'you' to 'we' at the end of my monologue. I remember that I didn't mean to say it, but when I registered that I had, I liked it; it felt right, it comforted me, I didn't feel anxious, and I didn't fret about it.

I also remember Tea's reaction when it registered. She tilted her head while eyeing me as if seeing me for the first time, the significance of the moment sinking in.

Tea needed some convincing, but not much. She loved The Place; when you love something, you want it to survive and thrive. She tried and put everything into The Place before realizing she couldn't do it alone, and then I came along.

3

After that momentous walk, and during the few weeks that followed, the change in their daughter made my parents stop and wonder with delight at the light that had flickered back on in her eyes. They would do anything to keep that light on; they would give everything within their power to prevent it from fading again.

I clearly remember Tea's outfit one evening later that autumn when she visited Big House to meet my parents and the Young Aunts. She wore an orange ankle-length flowy gypsy skirt and an off-the-shoulders asymmetric green sequined top; a light beige shawl with pink and orange flowers sewn into it completed the getup. The Young Aunts were fascinated with this chatty, bouncy burst of colors gliding into their midst. And my mother and father lovingly welcomed the source of their daughter's newfound purpose in life.

It was getting colder after sunset, but it was suitable for the balcony that evening. My mother fussed over Tea like a mother hen; she had made every cake, pie, and pudding in her recipe book. Tea had complained about her weight and how she'd started a new diet just that day, so she only had small portions of everything.

I thought Tea handled my aunts' interrogation beautifully.

"Why is a doctor—a gynecologist—instead of doctoring, selling books?!" exclaimed Aunt Feryal, genuinely perplexed.

"Too many years of ladies' hoo-hoos and babies popping out of them. I needed a change," Tea replied with the same practicality one would use when discussing the weather.

My scandalized mother busied herself topping up my father's glass with hot mint tea. He was fiddling with his cigarette pack, trying to get one out; I could see his grin, nonetheless. Gigi, my grandmother's faithful apprentice, understood perfectly well what had been said, and her laughter could be heard from the kitchen.

Feryal looked at Fatima, and both nodded in unison, deciding non-verbally that they liked this vulgar and colorful woman. My Young Aunts rarely left Big House; they preferred instead to reign over their home while friends and acquaintances flocked to them to pay their respect and allegiance. Nevertheless, in the years following that historic get-together, they made an exception in Tea's case. On more than one occasion, I would see them enter The Place, having made the trip from Big House, sitting on the Chesterfield, and calling for Saja to get them coffee and cookies. Frequently, ordering customers already sitting there to get up and make room. Naturally, Tea made a big deal of their visits and treated them like royalty. Yet, soon after they left, the famous 'This is a bookshop with coffee. Not a coffee shop with books!' was almost always voiced, albeit in a playful tone.

4

It took some time for the legal papers to be drawn and the financial part of the deal to be studied and assessed; my father hired his nephew, Aunt Asma's eldest son, my cousin Sami, to take care of the whole legal shebang. Sami had his firm's accountant review all The Place's accounts. A month or a little later, I was half-owner of The Place and Tea's new partner in the business.

I had my own money sitting in the bank that I never used. When I left my old job and moved back with my parents, and later when we all moved into Big House, I had nothing to use it on. There was nothing I wanted to buy, nothing to spend it on, except now. My father, however, had other plans. When I protested and told him I wanted to do this on my own and that I could manage, he said, "Please, Nuha, please, *habibti*. Let me do this for you." The meaning was not in the words; it was in his eyes. My father was a man of very few words, but I understood him well and more so than ever during that last year of his life.

Sunday 4 septemper

Tomorrow is stupid school.

My tummy really really hurts alot. I told mommy
and she smiled and she siad that maybe it is
because I am very iksited that school is tomorrow.
(mommy siad the word iksited means happy)

I am not iksited at all. School is stupid.

(I think that iksited is wrote like this

i k s i t e d) It is a hard word. I will ask mommy
about it, she siad I can ask about spelling of hard wods.

Maybe tomorow if I tell mommy my head hurts I
will not go to school.

Suzy broke her hand last year and did not come
to school for alot of days. I asked suzy in secont
grade if breaking your hand hurts and she siad just
a little.

The best 2 things that happened to me today

1. I got to play alot with my doll house.

2. I got to take Taesar for a walk alone. Mommy siad it is ok if I dont go far.

M is iksited about school not like me. He is meen and stupid.

Mommy came to my room and siad to get ready for bed because I have to get alot of sleep for school. I siad what if my tummy hurts tomorrow or may be my head and she siad a good night sleep will make it all beter and that it is ok if Taesar sleeps on my bed ☺

Daddy also siad good night to me.

I have to go now dear diary.

Good night.

CHAPTER 8

1

I open my eyes and listen. I know from the silence that he did not come home last night. At this time of the morning, Khaled is usually making a racket in the kitchen. He typically gets up an hour before me, so the bathroom is all mine by the time I stir. Today, there is nothing, only the distant cars and the random honking in the street below. I sit up in bed and look at my nightstand. I pick up the first of the framed photographs and kiss it. I pick up the other and do the same. I touch the notebook with the dandelion, keep my hand on it, and keep my eyes shut for a few seconds. I pick up my phone and check it. No messages or missed calls.

As I did with my regimen the night before, I go through my morning routine methodically and in quick succession. This is my process when I don't want to ruminate and over-think. I focus on the goal, and my goal this morning is getting ready for work, so I mechanically go about it and concentrate on my breathing, in and out. I leave my room thirty minutes later and head to the kitchen. I am making my morning cup of tea when I hear his key in the lock.

2

Khaled stands in the kitchen doorway, my back to him; I can't see him, but I sense his presence and smell his fresh scent. I don't turn to face him, but leave him to make the first move.

"Morning, beautiful. Did you miss me?" I can hear the

smile in his voice. Now I turn around and look at him, smiling too. I'm happy when he's happy.

Our perpetual point of conflict is that I always want him happy, and he, on the other hand, is perfectly content and satisfied with only occasional bouts of joy. I can even accept this were it not for the periods of intense grief and self-loathing that interrupt these intermittent bouts. My attempts to explain to him that he deserves to always be happy, continuously fail. And worse, on the rare occasions I try to explain, it makes him defensive and distant. We're caught in this catch-22 situation; when he's down, he's self-justifying and evades talking about it. On the other hand, when he's in good spirits, I'm afraid to confront him and ruin the mood.

This time it's no different; instead of finding a way to break the cycle, I say, "I missed this morning's commotion with the frying pans and the blender."

"Why, princess!! Lucky for you, we still have time. Please make yourself comfortable and watch a magician at work." He lifts me and places me on the kitchen stool.

When Khaled isn't around, I rarely have breakfast, just a cup of tea. When he is around, however, it's an elaborate affair. My eyes trail him around our kitchen; he reminds me of a skilled dancer, not a step out of place. I say nothing as he makes me pancakes and, for himself, his specialty omelet, made of eggs, parsley, and every kind of cheese in the fridge. Then I watch him squeeze oranges for me; he knows I like fresh orange juice and knows I rarely have it because it takes forever to get the smell off my hands. Today, I feel he's trying extra hard to please me. The blender comes out next for one of his protein smoothies. He has, in the past, tried to persuade me to try one of his concoctions, but to no avail. I will never touch them.

We sit opposite each other and eat. To say Khaled is a magician is an understatement. His pancakes are divine, light, and fluffy; I can easily eat a dozen. I have seen him create recipes and assemble tasty meals out of a few ingredients. On more than one occasion, whenever I tasted something fantastic that he had concocted, I suggested that he write the recipes down and collect them into a cookbook that he could later publish. But he has always brushed me off. This morning, I try again.

"They will sell, trust me; if not for the content, for your photo on the cover—you have the looks, and there's more than one lady who can't cook and who will choose your face from the cookbook stand," I say after I finish my pancakes and try, and fail, to steal a forkful of the omelet.

"I will work on the promotion for the book," I add. "We'll set you up for a book signing at The Place, and who knows, after that, the sky's the limit; TV, YouTube, and travel..." I try again and fail to snatch the last of the omelet.

He's looking at me and into my eyes and smiling. "I love you, Nona. I really do. And..."

"Don't call me that! Never! Please, Khaled," I blurt out, cutting him off mid-sentence. Eyes shut, I shake my head, trying to erase the picture that the name conjures. It is a knife gashing into me, a sharp knife, a clean slice into my heart.

"I know. God! I'm so sorry, *habibti*." He jumps off his stool and comes over to me.

I can't hear what he's saying. I'm doing my best not to fall into an abyss of my own making, one I haven't visited for some time now.

"I don't know what's come over me, Nuha *habibti*. I'm so sorry. I don't even know how it slipped," he says, holding me tight and rocking me gently.

I let a few seconds pass, then open my eyes and look at him. His features are contrite, and I believe him. I try not to overreact.

"And...?" I ask. I earnestly want to distract from his slip because I know it was a mistake he regrets, and I don't want to make a big deal of it. I don't want to ruin the morning for this gorgeous man.

"And...?" he asks me, genuinely puzzled.

"You said 'you loved me, you really did, and...?' Finish the sentence, big guy," I say, trying to put a little cheer into my voice.

"Oh! Yes. And you look totally gorgeous this morning."

"You think? You're not just saying it to butter me up so you can pick tonight's movie while clearly, it's my turn to pick?"

"Absolutely not!" he says, sounding shocked and indignant.

"Good, because I have a great one in mind," I reply. "Now get out of here. You're late." And with a quick look at my watch, I add, "We both are."

"Nuha, love, we're ok, right?" he asks.

"Always, you dummy, now get lost!" I answer.

3

Nona.

My name since my earliest memories until I stopped wanting it to be my name. My mother and father had some trouble abiding by my new rule, but ultimately learned to do just that. Grandmother never faced that problem because she was the only person who never called me by Nona, preferring to use Nuha, her mother's—my great-grandmother's—name instead. The pet name 'Nona' vexed my grandmother greatly. She insisted that Nuha was a beautiful Arabic name, meaning serenity, calm, and purity, and not old-fashioned like some claimed.

My aunts, their families, most of my school and college friends, and other distant relatives and acquaintances knew me by Nona. Some even kept calling me Nona, not understanding the big deal, even after the ban was imposed. Yet, they all learned the hard way to revert to my given name. I was pretty belligerent, taking offense and not answering or acknowledging anyone calling me by it. I might have been as such today, and probably would have been, if it was anyone other than Khaled.

I first met Khaled during my second year as an English major in college. He was in his first year studying civil engineering when Yara, a sweet English major and the birthday girl, first introduced him to the gang that momentous day. Khaled was her brother's friend, heard that it was her birthday, and came across our campus looking to celebrate with us. Ever since I laid eyes on him, he owned an exquisite sense of humor. Everyone liked him, and, in no time, he proved himself an integral part of the group. When we met, I was Nona, so for him, I was Nona from the start and all through college. Khaled and I met almost every day, except maybe during exams and college holidays. He became my backbone during my academic years. He was my confidant, shoulder to cry on, advisor, and best friend.

When I look back on those days, I wonder how I allowed what came next to happen, but it did happen. After graduation, our paths diverged, and I rarely saw Khaled for many years. On occasions, we would call, try to stay connected, and chitchat about this and that, but in the end, life took its toll. Although I tried to be there for him when his father passed away, it was a tough time for him then; he was distant and uncommunicative, and it wasn't an appropriate time for us to reconnect.

Then came my dark period, my bad days. Khaled heard, and he reached out to help me, but at the time, I was incommunicado, for loss of a better word. I was unreachable—would not and could not receive comfort or sympathy. Years later, I heard he was there during my grandmother's funeral and burial. Although I didn't see him then, I appreciated the sentiment and loved him for it. Soon after, I called him, and we talked. I cried on the phone that day; I remember he just listened silently as I wept. He didn't say a word; he understood that I was crying for my grandmother, for what happened before and since. He knew that I just needed to be heard, and he gave me exactly that, an ear, even if, at the time, I had little to say and many tears to spill. During that call, I asked him to call me Nuha and never to use Nona again. At the time, he didn't ask me why but promised me he would.

When my father, two years later, passed away, Khaled again attended the funeral and burial. This time he came to Big House after the three days of formal mourning had ended. Came in and commiserated with my mother and the aunts. I recall even Tea was there that day, and apart from the very faint pink in her hair, no other color except black was visible. He and I sat for a while and talked, and I told him about my new project. He was genuinely pleased for me, and from that day on, he started coming to The Place often. Baby steps at first, but little by little, we were rekindling our friendship. I told him everything. This time I will never let go of him. Whatever happens, not ever.

So, today, when the name Nona made an appearance, I knew, of course, that it was a slip of the tongue. I needn't even question it. He is, after all, my better half.

4

I hate being late, even as a business owner (or co-owner in my case). I'm a morning person, despite any previous sleepless nights. I make it a priority to arrive at least an hour before anyone else turns up. Typically, there are no customers at this early hour, but I always have a fresh pot of coffee ready just in case.

This morning, I open The Place, turn on the light, make the day's first pot of coffee, make myself a second cup of tea, and finally sit at my desk and fire up my computer. The antique desk I saw and fell in love with the first time I set foot in The

Place is my workplace now. Any other day I would have time to check my email, place our orders for the day, browse the internet, finish my tea, and start on another before Saja makes her appearance. But today, thanks to Khaled's pancakes, my day is off-kilter.

"Good morning," I say to Saja, who just came in and is fiddling with something at the register.

"Morning. You're early," she replies brightly, not looking my way, still busy with whatever it is that caught her attention.

Since the first day I started working at The Place, 'you're early' is a proclamation that comes from Saja's lips nine of every ten mornings. Years later, it has still to dawn on her that I'm always early.

"Yes, I am, aren't I?" I answer. "What are you doing there?"

"My charger. Have you seen it? Misplaced it somewhere." I see her race by me to the back.

I leave her to it and return to my first order of business; I answer my emails and send a few of my own.

"Found it!" Saja screams in delight from the back room. I hear the moving of boxes and the clattering of unidentified objects; I don't ask.

Second order of business, I check our website and social media pages and answer customer inquiries. I also text all registered customers about our three-day-only offer of 40% off all classics.

Twenty or so minutes later, Saja flounces out of the back room all smiles and with a bounce in her step now that she's found her charger. She heads for the shop's front window with a glass spray bottle in one hand and a rag in the other.

The third and most important order of business, which I am extremely excited about, is organizing the reading and book signing event for the up-and-coming children's book author Jamila S. For years now, book signings and book readings for local talent have become a regular occurrence at The

Place. I had ordered beanbags for the children's corner at the back of the store, where the event would take place. In addition to promoting it on our website and socials, I sent text invites to our regulars, and we're expecting a good turnout.

"They were supposed to deliver the beanbags yesterday. But I don't see them. No one called me to reschedule. Did someone call the shop?" I ask.

"Oh, you didn't hear, did you?" Saja responds, coming out from the back room with a watering can for the plants on the windowsill.

"Hear what? Why the delay?"

"You took off early yesterday. Big House day, wasn't it?" She enunciates it as an accusation.

"Saja, what happened?" I ask. Saja is a contrary person with a whimsical personality, sometimes with a quick temper and other times cool as a cucumber. I never know which persona I'm dealing with until I'm in the thick of it.

"They came at three yesterday but had the order mixed up." She recalls the events while dusting the bookshelves.

"Mixed up how?" I ask while bringing the purchase order back up on my computer to ensure I hadn't made a mistake. I hadn't.

"Madam T told them to take the beanbags all back." Clearly, Saja is having fun stretching the story to its limits, keeping me hanging.

"Yessss...?" I say impatiently, wishing I could sound indifferent and deprive her of the pleasure.

"Yes, what?" Saja says innocently.

"You know what?! I'll get the story from Tea when she's here. And you missed a spot of dust over there." I point to the table closest to the entrance while returning to my computer.

"Ok, ok!" she laughs. "Well, you see, this dreamy guy comes in, all tall, dark, and handsome, really tall, big muscles. I'm in love, I'll have you know!!"

I glare at her, and she continues, "So yes, he comes in, and following him are the delivery guys carrying the beanbags. It turns out they got the order wrong; you ordered one big one and four small ones, and they got four big ones and one small one."

"Oh, ok. I see, so wh…"

She waves my inquiry off; evidently, her narrative isn't over. "They take them to the back and try to fit them in the space, but they won't fit because it's too small, and they looked really ridiculous jammed together, blocking the door to the restrooms." Saja is back to dusting and shelving books. "Then Madam T came in from the back and exploded when she saw what they'd done and was about to start yelling, you know when she grabs the sides of her skirt and lifts them up?"

An image I have seen numerous times comes to mind of Tea lifting her skirt as if about to curtsy but, instead of curtsying, screaming her head off.

"What did she say?" I giggle.

"She was wearing a red dress, by the way, with green shoes. She looked like a fat ripe tomato!" Saja adds.

"Saja!! *Eayb ealiki*, shame on you," I reprimand but chuckle all the same.

She takes no heed and continues, "Anyway, she's about to attack them when tall, dark, and handsome comes over, apologizes, and promises to correct the mistake." Saja stops and thinks for a second. "He didn't say mistake, by the way, he said miscommunication."

Saja is cleaning the register and the gift-wrapping corner now and absently humming under her breath, "mis-com-you-nee-ka-tion…"

"Smitten with tall-dark-and-handsome, are we?!" I ask, intrigued.

"Oh! Turns out, tall-dark-and-handsome is the proprietor of the furniture store. He came with the delivery to introduce himself and get to know The Place. Then he confessed to Madam T that it was his mistake and so on and so forth and promised tomorrow—that's today—at three, he'll make sure we get the correct order," Saja concludes and beelines to the back room.

5

Tea rarely makes an appearance before the late morning, elevenish or thereabout, which is excellent as far as I'm concerned because after she enters, all focus on work bolts out the door. She's permanently encased in a bubble of hustle, bustle, and noise. The energy she brings into any room is like the music you want to stand up and dance to. She literally shines, and the verve she radiates is contagious. On more than one occasion, I find myself anticipating her arrival, knowing everything will be set right once she's here. I once heard Saja aptly describe Tea as 'Madam Fixit.' Whether she remedies situations by her loudness, rudeness, or both, no one cares; only the results matter.

Part of Tea's allure is her outrageous daily ensembles, and today, when she makes her entrance at ten minutes past eleven, she does not disappoint. Tea is in purple capri pants and a white shirtdress cut shorter at the front than at the back with puffy sleeves, high-heeled turquoise sandals, and two long bead necklaces, one turquoise and one purple. Contrary to Tea, my personal look is relatively subdued. Although I try for the simple and chic, I aim to shun attention rather than attract it. My signature look consists of dressy blue jeans with various tops; usually black, white, and shades of ivory, cream, and gray. Platform high-heeled sandals always complete my outfits. Khaled once commented that I own a zillion silk blouses in every shade of gray, which is not exactly true. They are not all silk; my closet also holds chiffon and lace, and the dark green or blue top may come out, but only occasionally.

"Good morning, gorgeous ladies," Tea declares as she crosses the threshold and throws perfunctory kisses Saja's and my way. Her oversized turquoise-rimmed sunglasses perch on her purple-streaked white hair.

She flings herself on the Chesterfield and gazes at me. "What's wrong with you?"

"Nothing!" I am genuinely taken aback by her question.

"Something is wrong; tell me," she persists.

"Nothing is wrong. Really, I'm fine," I say. I change the subject. "Saja just told me what happened yesterday."

Tea heaves herself up and strides to the back room, grumbling audibly, "I'll know what's wrong sooner or later."

"Nothing is wrong!" I follow her to her office. I change the subject again. "I predict an excellent turnout for the signing."

"Screw the signing! What's wrong with YOU, honey?" she asks, openly concerned.

I look at her, really look, long and hard. She knows me. She knows who I am and what I have been through. She knows everything! Why is she doing this today? Why must we go through this incessant question-and-answer session every few months? What is different about me today? Why do we have to go through this today, or any day for that matter?

"Why are you doing this now?" I ask. "Why do you keep doing this, Tea? Keep asking me how I am and what's wrong with me. Everything is wrong, Tea. Everything in this world is wrong!"

"But I thought you were getting better," she says, her voice placating, probably after hearing the emotion in mine. "Things are starting to look brighter and become right again. I can see it in your eyes, *habibti*."

"How can it ever be right again, Tea?" I start softly, but my tempo grows with every word. "It's been years, and it will never be right again. What you see is an act, Tea. I'm acting. I was fed up being a catatonic vegetable, so I decided to act happy and cheerful, get up every morning, get dressed, and get out. But my life isn't right! It's a shit show, and I can't wait for it to be over, so I can rest in peace from people who keep asking me how I am and what's wrong with me!"

Tea looks into my eyes, and I keep mine locked onto hers. She says nothing, so I continue, "And you know what ticks me the most, Tea? It's that you know all this. I have told you this. Every few months, we keep repeating this conversation. It's getting on my nerves. Aren't you tired too?"

"Oh honey, I was just trying to…"

I cut her off. "So, back to your question, what's wrong with me? The answer is everything and nothing. Everything, as in, all my life is shit. And nothing, as in today, there's nothing wrong more than the usual. So, are we done here?"

She doesn't say a word, just stares at a spot over my left shoulder. Then, finally, I hear the front door jingle and leave her standing there.

6

At five minutes to three o'clock in the afternoon, I'm working on our online purchases and on the phone with our delivery service discussing tomorrow's pick-up when a white van parks in front of The Place.

Saja jumps from behind the register and rushes to open the front door. A minute later, a delivery guy carries one of the small child-sized beanbags through the door and stands still, awaiting instructions on where to place it. I make my way to the back and usher the guy through; he is followed by a second carrying another beanbag. In a few minutes, all beanbags are arranged in a semi-circle at the rear of the shop but clearly visible from the entrance; two green, two blue, and the big beanbag is purple, giving a colorful backdrop to the interior, clearly marking the spot as the children's corner.

A third man stands by the door supervising the delivery. He is big and dark; indeed, Saja's description of these two attributes was spot on. As for handsome, it entirely depends on individual interpretation. The two delivery men are now outside; through the window, I see one light a cigarette, and the van obscures the other. I look through the front window as if for the first time, as if it's the most exciting view in the world and my life depends on it, anything to distract me from looking at the shop's door and the man standing there.

I smell him; it's a woody, spicy smell, a familiar scent, but as of now, it is his and only his scent. I feel him look at me. I feel his eyes piercing my skin. I know I must meet his gaze and acknowledge his presence. I hear voices and movement in my peripheral vision, yet only he is center stage; everything else is background hubbub. Still, I gaze straight on through the window, trying to delay the inevitable, if only for a few seconds, because once I look and my eyes meet his, I know there will be no turning back. All that I consider normal will disappear, and all the walls I have built, the defenses I have constructed over the years, will tumble over and wither away.

I hear words. It's Tea's voice; she's introducing him to me, she calls my name. The time has come. It's over. No delays are acceptable from this point forward. I must turn to face him. I put on a smile, and I summon the courage that has been hiding under layers of self-imposed barricades. I turn, and our eyes meet. And then he smiles. That's when it all starts to go wrong; just as I had anticipated, all my hard work unravels.

7

At a certain point in my life, I stopped living and started only existing. A tenacious determination to atone drove my existence at the time. It felt like I needed conscious effort to force my heart to beat and my lungs to breathe when it would have been so much easier to put a stop to it all. Following that hiatus came my decision to rejoin the ranks of the living but with self-imposed conditions. Self-preservation comes in many forms; surrounding oneself with predictability is one of those forms. Narrowing your circle of acquaintances and restricting newcomers is another.

Looking back at it, although stumbling on The Place was by sheer luck, I believe had my subconscious not calculated that the risk was minimal, I would not have chosen it as my comeback project. When I met Tea, I understood that she was a people person, and she would take the brunt of human interaction off anyone who worked with her. That attribute must have been a major player in my subliminal decision. By letting the people person in our partnership do her business, I'm left with minimal people-time and my work is done from behind the safe harbor of a computer screen. Running a bookstore is predictable and controlled, with little potential for surprises, or so I believed.

Now I stand on the precipice of an event horizon, on the brink of no return, about to put my hand into the hand outstretched, waiting for me to acknowledge its owner. A hundred questions assault my senses. Like what sets this man apart from the other customers we've had in the past? Why is he different from, say, the interior designer that Tea consulted a few weeks ago, the publishers we deal with, the electrician that came by last week, or the inspector the week before that? Or even the lost guy who asked for directions the other day? What exactly makes me take a longer, deeper whiff of his perfume? Why have I just registered the dimples on his cheeks? Why is he smiling? His head tilts slightly to the right as our eyes meet, and his hand engulfs mine.

He asks two questions that sum up all the questions I'm asking myself and several others that I still have to articulate. "Have we met before?" he questions. "Do we know each other?"

I know the answer to both questions, yet I only reply to the first, "No, I'm sure we've never met before."

I keep the answer to the second question to myself: Some part of us must have known of the other's existence even if we didn't know that we knew.

82

Monday 5 Septemper

Today was the first day of school. Miss Linda is our
teacher in grade 3.

My head hurt a little this morning and my
tummy to. Mommy siad that if it just hurts a
little it will go alone and that I should go to school
and she siad that if it starts to hurt alot I should
tell miss Linda and miss linda will tell my mommy
to come take me home.

Suzy sat next to me today. I like Suzy. She was
Sereena's friend in grade 2 but now she is my
friend because sereena is now Suha's friend. Suha
is new in my school. But sereena told suzy that
suha's mommy and sereena's mommy are best
friends and sereena's mommy told sereena that
she has to be suha's friend in school because suha is
new and she has no friends.

I like miss Linda. She is very pretty and she has
long hair. I wish my hair was long like miss Linda.
Suzy had long hiar in grade 2. But her mommy cut

it because her bother Mohanad put bublgum in it as a prank and her mommy had to cut it for her but siad that it will grow back. I hate boys. Boys are stupid and meen.

Miss Linda siad that we should learn very hard words in English in grade 3. She siad it is very important to improve our vocabulary. And she siad that I get the letter S and that I should tell the class on Wednesday 5 words begining with the letter S and I have to tell the class the meaning and use them in a sentenses. Suzy got the letter N. (I thnk the word vocabulary is a nice and hard word in the letter v)

I wanted the letter i because I want to tell them about the word iksited.

The best 4 things that happened to me today

1. Suzy is my best friend in the whole world.

2. My tummy and my head did not hurt me alot.

3. Miss Linda is the best teacher in the whole world.

4. My mommy siad that if I find 5 nice (very

hard) words with S in the dictionary she will tell me how to use them in sentenses.

My mommy siad that iksited does not start with i it starts with e and it is writen e x c i t e d and not i k s i t e d. ha ha ha ha at me ☺☺☺

I hear my mommy yelling for us to got to bed!! Good night dear diary ☺

CHAPTER 9

1

After parading an assortment of eligible young ladies by her son over the years, Areej, aka *Um Khaled*, was visibly surprised when her son announced that we were engaged. She had known me for years, the so-called 'best friend' of her perfect son. Areej was never convinced that a friendship could exist between a boy and a girl and once confessed as much to me over a cup of tea. This was during our university years. I drove to Khaled's house to pick him up in my car. I got my driver's license just that day, and we planned to celebrate with the gang. He was running late and shouted from his bedroom window for me to come up and meet his mother. I'd sooner stayed and waited in the car than sit and converse with Khaled's mother on cross-sex friendships, but he insisted, so I parked and did as I was told.

Um Khaled was a beautiful woman in her mid-forties, with long jet-black hair, hazel green eyes, and a patrician nose that fit her features perfectly, adding to her striking appearance. Khaled's parents had been separated since Khaled was four years old. His father lived and worked in Abu Dhabi and had an excellent relationship with his only son. They met on every holiday; his father would come to Jordan, or Khaled would fly to Abu Dhabi at least once a year to stay with his father, his father's new wife, and three younger half-sisters.

So, on that summer afternoon, when I had first set eyes on Areej, she did not hide it or try to be sly about it; she showed me straight off what Khaled meant to her. On every surface and on every wall stood or hung photos of Khaled. From a newborn baby to a grown man, I could see several smiling Khaleds and many serious-looking Khaleds. Khaled riding a tricycle, a bicycle, a plastic toy car, and a horse. Walking beside his mommy, swimming in a pool, and swimming in the sea. A picture of a man I didn't recognize holding a toddler Khaled upside down by his foot. Several other images of him smiling in graduation caps, reading a book, and eating an apple. I saw baby Khaled on a swing, on a seesaw, in summer clothes, and swaddled in winter clothes. On the walls also hung framed report cards; luckily, Khaled was a bright kid because even if he wasn't, the report cards would have been displayed regardless of what they divulged. Likewise, his swimming trophies, tennis trophies, and medals of every color and description adorned corner tables and shelves.

Areej caught me ogling her home exhibition and didn't comment, just left me to it. Meanwhile, I could feel her eyes weighing and checking me out, trying to discern if I was good enough, pretty enough, and worthy enough of her treasure. Had I told her that she needn't bother, that I was only Khaled's friend and that I was not interested in her son in any other way, she wouldn't have believed me. In her mind, who wouldn't be interested in her perfect son in that way and in every other conceivable way?

"Nona *habibti*, I heard Khaled mention you before," she said coolly but politely. "Sit, sit. I'll make tea—be right back."

"Don't bother with tea, Aunty, no need. We'll be leaving in a minute."

"Nonsense *habibti*, and please call me Areej. Aunty makes me feel ancient!"

"Thank you, Aun... Areej." I was so uncomfortable and just wished Khaled would finish whatever he was doing inside and get out so we could leave.

"So, tell me, Nona, you're studying English, right?" I heard her words and the rattling of crockery from the adjoining kitchen.

I followed her to the kitchen. "Yes, English. Starting my third year this fall, *inshallah*, God willing."

"Third year? Oh, I see. Hmm," she said. Clearly, she was only 'seeing' what she wanted to see. "Khalloodeh will be starting his second year."

"Yes, I know," I replied, knowing full well where she was going with this.

"So, you are what...? Twenty?"

"Twenty-one this December," I chirped. My birthdays have always been my favorite day of the year. I couldn't mention one without making a big deal.

"Khalloodti is only nineteen."

"I know," I said, trying to keep the cheeriness in my voice. "We're best friends, Aunty. I'm the one who arranged his last surprise birthday party."

"Friends...!" she scoffed, busying herself with pouring the hot tea into two glasses.

"Best friends," I corrected her. 'Where are you, shithead?!' I thought but didn't say.

"What a silly notion. I was just a few years older than you now when I had Khaled," she said matter-of-factly as if that explained everything.

"Oh, not me! I won't be getting married or having children before I'm well into my thirties."

"Then why are you wasting my Khaled's time?" she asked, bewildered.

"We are just friends, Aunty, that's all," I said. I tried to infuse as much calmness in my words as possible, but clearly, my point wasn't getting through. Areej couldn't grasp that anything other than landing a husband could be going through any young lady's mind. I wanted to assure her that I cared for her son as a friend with no hidden agenda.

But before I could convey this message or even try to, in stepped Khaled, dressed to the nines, hair wet and combed back, smelling of aftershave, utterly oblivious to the fact that he lived in a shrine, and the keeper of said shrine was wholly detached from his friends and his life.

2

Decades later, I leave the passenger seat and wait for Khaled to lock the car, and we both walk to the front doorstep. Friday is our weekly pilgrimage to my mother-in-law's house. We ring the bell and hear her heels clack on the tiles. She opens the door in a dark blue sarong-like dress and high heels. Areej wears heels everywhere, and I don't remember ever seeing her in flats. She even owns high-heeled slippers for home use, like the silver strappy pair she has on today. Now in her sixties, she is still as striking as the first day I rested my eyes on her. Her eyes have the same piercing intensity as they did back then, her figure kept, her hair still jet-black but shorter and skimming her shoulders, and her features still preserving their previous splendor. When Tea once asked her flat out if cosmetic injectables played a role in her maintenance regimen, she firmly and adamantly denied it, and attributed her radiance to maintaining a healthy diet and living a fulfilling and joyful life. Nevertheless, I suspect my mother-in-law is fibbing.

"*Hayati* Khaled. I missed my baby." Areej coos and melts into her son's arms.

I brace myself for a long afternoon of the same sentiments. Areej fawning over Khaled, indulging his every whim and laughing at his every utterance, no matter how mind-numbing. I am also my mother's only child, but I have never received this kind of devotion. Khaled's face meets mine, and he reads my expression, although I try desperately to hide it. He calls it my 'involuntary-quizzical-eyebrow-lift' and laughs in return with a wiggle of his own eyebrows.

Finally, he mouths questioningly, "Jealous?!"

"Yeah, right!!" I mouth back.

3

Areej and I are not the tête-à-tête kind of people, but we did have a one-time heart-to-heart. This happened one late Friday afternoon in her home after Khaled and I married. Khaled was away on a training course, and I decided not to break with tradition and went to my mother-in-law's alone. Later that day, she suggested we have tea on the terrace. Her apartment building is on a hill overlooking a considerable part of west Amman; the view is breathtaking in the evenings. It was a late October evening, and the weather was starting to get chillier. Still, we decided to stay out in the fresh air and wrapped ourselves in blankets.

I wasn't oblivious to the history of Khaled's parents and their short and turbulent marriage, but I never heard the account from the principal player herself. Instead, I heard it from the son who was too young when the separation took place and obviously loved his parents equally and thus was unprejudiced. I remember that she told me many things that evening. I remember her telling me that a week ago marked the twelfth anniversary of *Abu Khaled's* death. I also recall her telling me that having Khaled was the only bright thing that came out of that sordid ordeal. Then she told me all about the sordid ordeal. She talked, and I listened, did not ask questions, and did not interrupt. She was reminiscing, and I knew from experience the importance of lending an ear to those in need.

"I got married exactly three months after finishing dental school. My betrothed was an associate professor in the faculty of medicine here in Jordan. He saw me while I was still an undergrad and back home from Cairo for a visit, and I guess he became infatuated. He asked my father for my hand right after graduation; we were only a few days back from Cairo when Murad knocked on our door. I was delighted with my older, handsome, well-to-do associate professor from a well-known family. I envisioned myself as a bride in white, the talk of the town, and the object of envy of all my friends. I dreamed of a fairytale wedding and a honeymoon in Italy. I was delighted to be the first of my friends to get hitched. My dear father was a levelheaded man; he was pleased for me. Who wouldn't want his daughter to be married to a good man from a respected family? But I remember he told me to slow down, to take my time, to think well about what I was doing, and that there was no rush. But obviously, I didn't listen to him and was unwavering in my decision. One of my friends told me the same; I thought she was jealous. I wanted to marry Doctor Murad, my knight, and I fancied myself head over heels in love with him. I had an enchanting three months of an engagement, during which he peppered me with gifts almost daily. Huge bouquets of red roses, silly stuffed animals that, at the time, I thought were delightful. I had little time to really contemplate what I was plunging into. Instead, I was busy with getting fitted for my bridal gown, wedding plans, flower arrangements, guest lists, photographers, big decisions such as wedding bands, decorating my new apartment, and purchasing my trousseau; I hardly had time to sleep, let alone think. Thinking back, I don't know how I could have done all that in three months! To this day, I am amazed at my tenacity during that brief period all those years ago. Finally, the big day came, and it was a magical event, then off on my honeymoon."

Areej fell silent and hesitated, not knowing how to continue. Sometimes, talking about something diminishes its enormity. She was searching for the right words to make me understand, to communicate to me the immensity of that pivotal time of her life. "And like they say: *Rahat alsakra wa ja'at alfikra*, I sobered up, and it hit me!" she said, and I smiled inwardly; it was one of my grandmother's favorite aphorisms.

She continued, "I didn't know him or anything about him, Nuha." Even after all those years, I could see the pain was still there and still smarting; the look in her eyes pierced my heart. I took her hand in mine but said nothing. "I was in love with the idea of being in love and playing house. I romanticized the idea of being married. I never slowed down to think about what being married entailed. I was too young to understand, too naïve to take the advice that a handful of people tried to give me before it happened, and too stubborn to admit that I might have made a mistake and rushed into it. So, in the beginning, I soldiered on."

She gazed into the distance, into the Amman night. I thought the narrative was over after minutes of silence, so I didn't push her to continue. Instead, I watched the Amman lights flicker and twinkle. We listened to the sounds of distant cars, a dog's faint bark, and a faraway ambulance siren. Then, just as she'd stopped, she suddenly picked up again.

"Nobody prepared me for what was coming. We used to talk, you know, my friends and I, the girls, about marriage and men and, you know... sex, but... honestly, Nuha! No one prepares you for it. How awkward it is and, well, you know, how painful!! Our first night was... I don't know how to describe it—a tragedy! No one tells you what to do when you wake up one day next to a strange man, what to say to him, how to react. The extent of my knowledge of this man was the few times we went out together; he spoiled me rotten and talked about nothing, just vague subjects. I can't even remember exactly what we talked about, except my favorite song and best movie. He went with me to look for furniture for our home once, then he said he trusted my judgment and taste and that I should go on without him. Money was no object; he gave me carte blanche and told me to decorate as I saw fit. At the time, I thought it was flattering, but later I realized that he just wasn't interested. It's so strange, Nuha. I'm telling you all this now and feel like an idiot. You might be thinking, how could I have let this happen to me? But it felt right and normal at the time, and it was how things were done and are still sometimes done! Am I rambling?"

Who was I to pass judgment on anyone? Who was I to

criticize anyone's actions? "You can ramble as much as you want, Areej. I have nothing to do and nowhere better to be," I told her with a smile. We had settled a while back on the name 'Areej.' She didn't like 'Aunty' and was unyielding on the subject.

"The most painful thing a person can do is to act happy when she is anything but. To act like things are exactly right and perfectly normal when in reality, my entrails turn to mud whenever I muse on what I have done." She fell quiet again; it was as if she was giving me time to digest little by little her story. "Nuha, you know what? No one forced me to marry a man I hardly knew. No one pushed me to do anything I didn't want to do. I can't even blame circumstances for my nightmare. It wasn't like I had no prospects; I was a stunning beauty and still am, *alf min yetmanaani*, I'm a catch!" She stopped, looked at me, and laughed heartily. I giggled, too; I have always admired my mother-in-law's assurance and self-confidence in her beauty, even now, well into her sixties.

Areej started abruptly again, but this time with the air of a judge passing the final ruling. "I am to blame. If I had been forced to do it, I would have had someone or something to condemn, but that was not the case. I was naïve, maybe, but I went to the best schools and to the best university; I had no excuse. I was too obstinate to listen to good advice when it was handed to me, end of story."

We sat in silence for a while. It's funny what trivial details people can sometimes remember. Areej was seated to my left that night, and I recall a spider descending from the ceiling and dangling to my right. It wasn't too close to cause distress or far enough for comfort. However, I was cautious not to make sudden movements and disrupt that meaningful conversation with my mother-in-law. I recall silently urging the spider to remain still and not spoil this rare heart-to-heart.

"And I soldiered on, Nuha. I persevered! I was under no illusion that Murad was any happier than I was, but I had a distinct feeling that he considered the situation 'normal'; all new brides were initially shy and had little to say. He had a beautiful young wife who would eventually get used to married life; all would be well in the end. When we returned from our honeymoon, he was all smiles and talked to no end about the hotels we stayed in, in Rome, Florence, and romantic Venice! When the photos were developed, I saw tens of pictures of me smiling. Still, I didn't recognize myself in any of them. I smiled at my friends and showed them the photos, they oohed and aahed, and I made perfectly sure that they left convinced that I was the happiest and luckiest bride to ever exist." Areej got up with no preliminaries and headed inside for the kitchen. I unswaddled myself from my blanket and followed behind. She was at the kettle putting in more water and stood there waiting for it to boil.

"More tea?" she asked, and I nodded my assent. It was then that I saw the tears in her eyes. After all the years that had passed, the pain was still there. An immeasurable sensation of sorrow for my mother-in-law gripped my heart.

I've often heard it said that time heals all wounds. From my experience, it takes a strong person to keep hold of pain and painful memories because it's how we learn. With time we discover how to control them and not let them control us. We learn to live at peace with them, find ways to keep the demons in specially constructed dungeons in our consciousness, and pass by them whenever we feel strong enough to handle them. We may observe these memories, we may reflect on them with other people, and in some cases, we can deliberate with them in private. We peek at them from well-constructed peepholes, but we should never let them out by opening the dungeon doors.

Back on the terrace, steaming hot tea in hand, Areej resumed, "A feeling of envy stabbed at my heart when Sawsan, who studied with me in Cairo, told me that she was about to open her own dental practice. You remember Sawsan. You met her, right? Anyway, till then, I had yet to consider my degree, all the years spent away from home, living in a different country to get an education. What had I been thinking?! What possessed me?! Do you know something, Nuha? To this day, I have no answers!"

I was still in tune with Areej, but my eyes roamed the vicinity for the creepy-crawly.

Noticing this, I heard her inquire irritably, "What are you doing?!"

"Nothing! Go on, Areej, please. I'm listening."

"I wonder what Khaled is doing?" she speculated out loud.

I knew I had lost her and could have kicked myself. I had to go and fuck it up, and because of a spider, no less! I had to think fast and lure her back in, so I asked, "I'm sure having baby Khaled made things better at the time, right?"

"And when, may I ask, are you two planning to make 'things better'?" she snapped back. Clearly, my ruse had bombed. But I should have known that, confidants or not, no way would Areej let an opportunity pass her by without bringing up the subject dearest to her heart, Khaled's highly awaited babies. Areej stood up again, cup of tea in one hand and her blanket tucked under the other arm, turned with a theatrical flip of her hair to show finality, and disappeared inside.

Well, at least she didn't add the dreaded 'neither-of-you-is-getting-any-younger' proclamation that usually followed the baby question. Still, before I could celebrate the fact, I saw her reappear. "And by the way," she said, "neither of you is getting any younger!"

I wanted to open my mouth to say something, anything, but that was when I felt it crawl up my leg.

4

Today, Areej makes *Mansaf**. I set the dining table while Khaled is in the kitchen with his mother. I hear hushed voices, and I hear the click of high heels, as well as the occasional burst of giggles. When mother and son are together, I sometimes keep my distance and give them time to catch up. I know Khaled wants to update his mother on his pet project, the gym, which she will undoubtedly find fascinating. When it comes to her son, Areej is an infatuated halfwit; he's her world, she hangs on his every word, and she smiles after every trivial remark. However, in other aspects of her life, my mother-in-law is a success story and a pillar of her profession. After her divorce and becoming a single parent, and regardless of her rough earlier start along her professional career path, she now owns a very successful dental practice in the heart of Amman. Apart from her clinic, she is on the committees of several charities, is socially dynamic, and her presence is coveted at many community events. And although I'm not an expert on such affairs, Tea assures me that Areej is the real deal.

I lay out the plates and cutlery. I arrange the water glasses next to every place setting. I hear a message notification and feel my phone vibrate in my back pocket. Table set, I sit down and look at my screen; it's a WhatsApp message. The message is from a number I still have to assign a name for, but a number I recognize, nonetheless. I know it because I spent a significant amount of time yesterday contemplating dialing it. As if a naughty secret or a covert plan, I looked at it only when alone, tried dialing, stopped, did it again, and then thought better of it.

And today, here I am. I stare at the number but do not open the message. Instead, as if to delay gratification, I wait. I hear mother and son approaching the dining area. I slip the

---

* Mansaf, the national dish of Jordan, is a traditional Arab dish made of lamb cooked in a sauce of fermented dried yogurt (jameed) and served with rice.

phone back into my pocket and stand up abruptly like a badly behaved child caught doing something mischievous. Khaled enters with the *Mansaf* platter in hand. Areej follows, carrying a bowl of *Jameed*.

The rest of the afternoon is a blur. I do, I hear, I speak, I register that we eat, I help Areej clear away the table, wash up the dishes, and put away the dishes. Khaled makes tea; we have tea. But during all that, anticipation builds inside me, a kind of guilty expectation, a wicked pleasure that distracts me from the happenings around me. The idiom 'floating on air' is not far from describing what I feel. But there is a difference; while that expression conveys happiness and lightheartedness, my heart is so heavy I find it hard to breathe.

5

I turn my bedside lamp on and turn off the main light switch. I sit on my bed. I look at my nightstand. I pick up the first of the framed photographs and kiss it. I pick up the other and do the same. I get under the covers and pick up the notebook with the dandelion. I read four pages, close it, and return it to where I found it. I pick up my phone off the nightstand and brace myself for what's to come. I open WhatsApp, scroll to the message from the number without a name, and tap on it.

> Kefek sitti? 1:35 PM

[How are you, ma'am?]

It is a message from a new contact; I get two options: BLOCK or ADD. I tap on ADD. I get two options: 'Create new contact' or 'Add to existing contact.' I tap on 'Create new contact.' I type in his first name: Zaid.

I do not reply. I switch off the light. I wait for sleep to come. It takes a while for it to arrive.

Wednesday 7 Sep.

My mommy is the best mommy in the whole world. My mommy helped me with my S words. And today is school I did very good in English class.

Yesterday was very hard. I worked all day after school looking in the dictonary for 5 words in English that begin with S. there were 5 hunderd billion words and I only wanted 5!! I liked many S words that sounded really really cool. And I liked alot long words that really sounded nice and some were very hard to read. My mommy helped me and we laughed and laughed. It was so much fun.

My words are:

1. Scrumptious

It sounds really cool and it means (yummy)

Sentense: My grandma cooks scrumptious food!

Miss linda siad it was a very good word.

2. Superstition

It means believing in the unnatural things and

accepting them as true... I did not understand and then my mommy told me the word in arabic and then I understand it. I think it is a funny word to say! ☺

Sentense: I like black cats they are cute, and I don't believe in the superstition that they are bad luck.

Miss linda siad that my sentense is very sofisticated (another very good S word ha ha ha ☺)

3. Sheepish

My favorite of my words!!! It reminds me of a sheep haha! It means showing or feeling embarrassed.

Sentense: I gave my mommy a sheepish smile before I told her that I broke the vase.

Miss linda siad bravo to me on that sentense (my mommy helped me with all the sentenses but I did not tell miss linda that but I did give her a sheepish smile!) ha ha ha ☺☺

4. Sanctimonious

Very hard word means being a hypocrite and

showing that you are better than other people. My mommy siad that it is very hard for grade 3 but I love it and I siad please please please! And she siad ok ok ok!

Sentense: (I wanted) M is sanctimonious.

Mommy laughed and laughed and laughed and siad that poor M is a sweetheart and I should find some other sentense that the rest of the class can relate to.

(Other sentense) He judges others and does the same, I consider him to be rather sanctimonious.

Mommy siad that's better.

Miss linda just siad: waw! (and I think I saw a sheepish smile)

5. Succinct

(I wanted the word Scandalize, but mommy siad please please Faten, use Succinct) Succinct is my mommy's favorite word in the whole English language she siad.

It means brief and concise writing or expression.

(the word Concise is very beautiful, if I had the letter C I would use it)

Sentense: The students were asked to write succinct summaries of the lesson.

Miss linda did not look sheepish, she looked happy with me.

The best things that happened to me today

1. My mommy is the best! I love her

2. I think M forgot all about this diary and does not come inside my room to look for it any more ☺

3. My 5 words were the best 5 words in all the world

4. I love writing in english

5. I am very good in english

6. Suzy is my best friend and her words were good to

Good night ☺

CHAPTER 10

1

I look at my face in the mirror. At a certain point in the not-too-distant past, I could not tolerate this face. Although recently—I cannot confidently pinpoint the day—I started once again to accept what I see. Today, for the first time, I notice something new. I see the lines on my forehead and at the outer corners of my eyes. This surprises me, though not their presence as much as the intensity of my sudden and unexpected care that they exist and my concern as to what to do about it.

I stand in my underwear and gaze into my closet. Tens of hanging tops and blouses stare back at me. I have a system, a foolproof one, on how to choose my outfit every day. Today, my system is a bust. I scrutinize the light gray blouse in my hand; it will not do. I start sifting through my wardrobe piece by piece and panic when I realize it needs expanding. My panic subsides somewhat when my roaming eyes land on a flowy bright blue satin long-sleeve blouse hanging at the very end of the rail. The notched round neckline shows cleavage but not too much of it. The asymmetric hem adds a touch of bohemian quality. The piece was a present from Tea on my last birthday. Her failed (at the time) attempt to, using her words, 'add color to my dull (and boring, I think she said) sense of style.' It is still new, hanging in my closet. Its color, before today, wasn't something I would normally contemplate. Today, the color lures me toward it.

On my way out of the apartment, with Khaled two steps behind me, I suddenly stop, and he collides with my back.

"I'm so sorry, sweetie," I say. "I forgot something. So you go, don't wait. I'll see you later." I smile and kiss his cheek.

"Take care, *habibti*." And he's off. Something is on his mind. I can sense it but don't have the inclination to think about it. Not now.

I'm back in my bedroom rummaging through drawers. I finally find it. A small pink vanity case, another unused present of two or maybe three birthdays ago. I open it and delve into the contents. I find what I need and walk over to the closet mirror. I screw open the mascara and examine the wand. It doesn't seem too dry and looks in working order. I steady my hand, take a deep breath, hold it, and apply mascara to my upper lashes, a maneuver I had forsaken for many years. To my amazement, I succeed on my first try, screw the mascara shut, and examine the result.

2

The reckless pangs of vanity that have unexpectedly taken over my morning are so uncharacteristic and very worrying. I analyze the reason for this behavior while driving, but I know it is futile because I already know the reason. Pretending that I don't know is time wasted. In The Place, I sit silently at my desk, staring at my computer, and try to control my breathing. My cold tea sits next to my silent phone.

Saja finds me in this state.

She either doesn't notice that I'm staring at a blank screen or does notice but doesn't comment except for her usual "You're early."

I ignore her. She goes along with her daily routine with no other word or glance. Then, at fifteen minutes to ten, our first customer arrives, a hurried-looking woman hunting for a present for her daughter's friend. She prattles on to no one in particular about how she must take the gift to school because she forgot to buy it yesterday and so forth. I stand up and start to suggest something, but before I take a step, she picks a random book from the young adult section and walks to the register. I sit back down.

I turn on my screen and start typing. I hear arguing coming from the front of the store. It seems that Saja is taking longer to gift-wrap the book than the hurried woman is willing to tolerate. Saja explains why it is vital for the wrapping to be done expertly and how she's been doing this forever. I shut them both out and continue typing. Silence follows. Minutes fly by, and an hour passes with my eyes glued to the computer. Then an explosion of sounds and colors.

The first thing Tea notices once through the door is my blue blouse. The complex emotions on her face in the few seconds it takes her to scurry over from the entrance to my desk show amusement on the one hand and, surprisingly, a touch of concern on the other. But before she can comment or joke about it, she screams, "Oh MY GOD!" when her eyes land on my screen. Her hands close over her mouth in mock astonishment.

"What?!" I exclaim, bemused. "I always shop online."

"Yes, you do, for the drapes you insist on wearing. But this! This is different. Red?! RED! A red dress!!! Sajaaaaa! *Ta'ali shufi*, come look!" she booms.

My grandmother used to aptly describe people like Saja with '*bdha ors torqus fih*,' as if always on the lookout for something to get worked up about. Saja rushes over, happy to oblige. She stares into the screen and offers her own faux shock reaction. She even goes as far as touching my forehead to tell if I've developed a fever. I shoo her hand off and stand up. "Yes, yes! You are both hilarious. HA HA."

Tea saunters off to the back room, muttering that I almost gave her a heart attack and that I'm going to be the end of her. Saja looks me up and down with narrowed eyes and asks suspiciously, "Sexy red dress? Hmm."

Alone again, I look at the item under discussion. Is this what I want to be? Sexy? Just moments ago, I felt out of sorts and spaced out; I needed something but didn't know what it was or why I was looking for it and couldn't put my finger on it until now. Saja put it all into just one word—sexy. I don't feel defensive; I don't feel I want to admonish her for saying it. Had she said it months ago, I'm pretty sure I would have. Now, I feel relief. I quickly add the item to my shopping cart and proceed to checkout.

3

I open WhatsApp. I read the two-word message he sent. Still unanswered. I scrutinize his profile picture. It's a selfie; I know this because I can see his mobile phone reflected in his mirrored aviator sunglasses. He's smiling; one corner of his mouth rises slightly higher than the other. One dimple is somewhat deeper on one cheek than on the other. A five-o'clock shadow adorns his chin, face, and neck. Perfect teeth; an exceedingly small gap separates his two front teeth, barely noticeable, but I still remember it from our first encounter. I thought to myself then, 'Perfect imperfection.' His hair is black, short, and thick, combed back off the forehead, and the damp texture suggests a hair product keeps it well-behaved and in place. How will it feel between my fingers? An alarming thought! What business do my fingers have going anywhere near this man? Let alone play with his hair. Play with his hair! Where did that thought even come from? Play!?

I try to control my breathing, which has lost its normal rhythm and has become irregular for some reason. I intentionally take a long, deep breath, hold it in, and release it slowly. I close my eyes and find myself meditating on the one feature this photo does not show. When we met and shook hands, my eyes locked with his. Blacker than black irises flecked with a lighter shade of brown, surrounded by whiter than white sclera. Upturned, long, and thick lashes encase the black and white within. Those lashes are his most striking feature.

Zaid is tall, and he is dark, and although I cannot be sure precisely by how much, he is at least ten years younger than I am. Although he is not handsome, he's the embodiment of sexy. He has captivated my imagination and invaded my dreams, and I have no idea what to do about it.

And, just like that, as if he senses me examining his WhatsApp profile picture, I see him come 'online.' I feel my heart flutter, stop, and start beating again when I see 'typing...' appear under his name. The seconds that follow are excruciatingly exquisite. I wait. In a few moments, when he sees the two ticks instantly turn to blue, he will know that I've been online waiting for it, but I don't care. I wait.

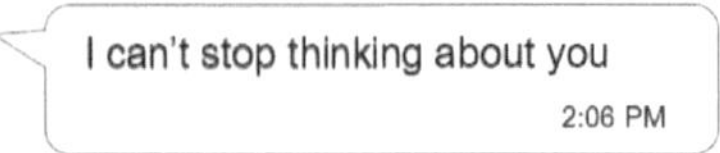

I stare at the statement. I avert my eyes. I look again. Sensations I've never felt before course through me. Describing them will be ineffective because I lack the words. This is new. I will deal with this later. For now, I will leave it, like the one before it, unanswered. I turn off my phone.

An unsolicited image of Khaled comes into my mind. The person who knows me best. He can help me. But Khaled is the last person I want to think about right now. I decide to turn off both the image and the associated thought.

The guilt comes in waves and from two different directions, one from my past and another from my present. I'm crushed between the tides and don't know how to escape.

4

Two kids, an older boy, probably six years old, and his younger sister, sit on two small beanbags, each with a book. The girl reads or makes a show of doing so, and the boy gazes at the pictures in his chosen book with facial features that show utter boredom. Their mother, on the big beanbag, is on her mobile, texting. I witness all this while shelving new books in the children's section, anything to divert me from gazing into blank computer screens or unanswered, inflammatory WhatsApp messages.

I call Jamila, the star of our upcoming event. I chitchat with her for a few minutes and reiterate the date and time of the book signing. I needn't have; she's as excited as we are and hasn't forgotten, nor is she likely to. I hang up and realize that the whole mundane call was a complete waste of time and unnecessary. I hope that Jamila doesn't think that I'm losing my mind. Little does she know that the call is only a distraction from my deleterious thinking.

At a few minutes past three o'clock in the afternoon, one hour exactly after the exquisitely guilt-loaded message came, the door opens. I turn and look in that direction and see a delivery man, with white roses and red lilies instead of a head, standing at the open entrance. Saja shoots toward him, frees him from his burden, and thanks him profusely. A beautiful arrangement of flowers now rests on the table between the Chesterfield and the two armchairs. Tea occupies the settee, and Saja and I the two armchairs. We study the bouquet.

"Who's it from?" Tea asks.

"No card," Saja answers.

"Must be a satisfied customer who forgot to write his name," Tea suggests with pride and a wide smile.

"Or a secret admirer," Saja suggests slyly and sends a suspicious look my way.

I ignore the insinuation, say nothing, look at no one, and only admire the arrangement. I already discerned the sender the second I saw the flowers at the door. I feign ignorance while guilt-ridden pleasure builds inside me and threatens to explode.

Back at my desk, I find a message on my phone. I know who sent it, so I decide not to open it. This man's onslaught is relentless, and I need all my wits about me. Saja hovers too close for comfort. Duster in hand, she cleans dirt-free shelves and dust-free surfaces. I feel her eye me warily, but she says nothing, and I act like I don't notice. Then I hear indiscernible mutterings from her; I turn and fake surprise as if I just saw her there.

"Did you say something?" I ask.

"How's Khaled?" she asks in lieu of an answer to my question, in a tone that's not so much an inquiry as an accusation. 'Remember Khaled,' she means. Am I making too much out of this? Is this just my guilt leading me to overanalyze the most basic queries?

An oblivious Tea saves me from finding answers to Saja's or my own musings by making a beeline from the back office door to the beanbags. "Guess who's getting a divorce?" she says before her backside touches the purple one.

5

I stand in my kitchen and lean on the counter. I'm alone. Khaled called a few minutes ago and told me he would be late. I didn't ask why or for how long. It is dark outside. I concentrate on the vase's reflection in the window facing me. An odd combination of bizarre thoughts runs through my mind. Mundane thoughts, such as, why can't I see my face reflected in the window? And, how far do I have to move so my head's reflection appears in the window? More substantial contemplations, such as, what do I do with the messages I received from a specific someone? For how long can I ignore someone before they lose interest? Do I want a certain someone to lose interest and leave me in peace? Or do I want this person to pursue what he's doing until I decide what I want to do about him? And finally, the most critical consideration of all. I'm married. He must have seen the ring on my finger.

My phone lies next to me on the counter. I take a deep breath and pick it up. I go to WhatsApp and open it. Two new messages await, not just one.

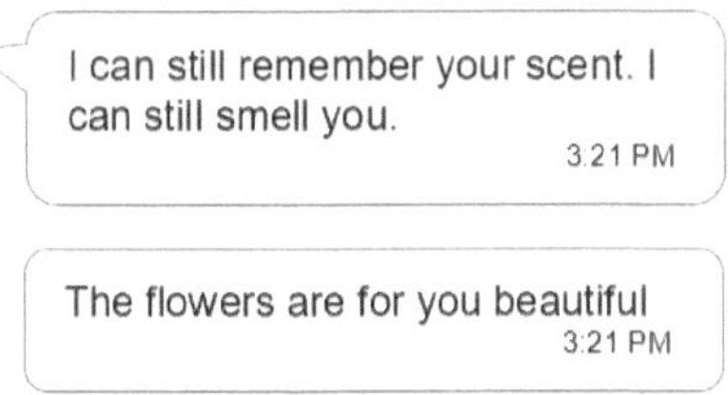

I read and reread them. They both go unanswered like the two messages preceding them. His attitude disturbs me; it's very reckless and presumptuous of him to send me such messages. But more disturbing is that I like it.

Friday 16 Sep.

Today is the weekend!! NO school ☺

I don't hate school any more. I don't like school.
I am neutral about school. My mommy siad that
the word (neutral) means indifferent, that I feel
nothing about school. But she also siad that she
hopes that I will start to like school like she did
when she was small like me.

I have not wrote in this diary for a long time (9
days). Because I am studying a lot. I must get
good grades in school this year. My daddy and
mommy siad to us that if we get good grades
they will take us to aqaba to swim in the red sea.
So I am studying and studying but I am afraid M
will not study and will not get good grade and we
will not go to aqaba in the mid term break because
M is stupid.

M asked daddy why is it called red sea is it
because the sea is red? (stupid M!) Daddy siad no

the sea is not red it is blue like all the seas.

The best thing that happened to me today is that (maybe) we will go to aqaba ☺☺

Sorry I havent wrote alot in you dear diary. I promise I will do it more. Good night now.

I cant sleep. why is it called the red sea?

Maybe red fishs? Or shark attacks and lots of blood?!! ☹

I hope our hotel has a swimming pool...

CHAPTER 11

1

I had the dream again. It's been a while. But tonight was the night. I am alone on the shore; the dog was not there this time. I felt abandoned and so alone. The water was red but icy; it lapped over my bare feet and made me shiver. And the sky turned very dark, very fast...

I surface suddenly. I try to concentrate—the vibrations. The vibrations wake me—the near hum of the mobile on the nightstand. My eyes are closed, but I sense it's still dark outside. The hum continues—it doesn't want to stop. This is not a message alert. This is a call. My hand rises and lands on the phone; the vibration persists. I pick it up and bring it to my face. My eyes try to center on the single word on the screen. My vision swims and my heart beats faster as the word comes into focus. Gigi.

I sit bolt upright. Nothing good comes from a call in the early morning hours, especially from Big House. I answer, listen for a few seconds, respond with "I'm on my way," and terminate the call. I take a deep breath and try to calm down. No need to panic. This is not the first time, and Gigi knows the drill. I get out of bed, look at the nightstand, kiss my fingertips, brush them over the dandelion on the notebook, and enter the bathroom. I wash and dress in less than ten minutes. I stand in the kitchen and look at the microwave's digital clock. 4:36.

The balcony light is on; I walk to the glass door and look through. Khaled sits with his back to the sliding door, earbuds in, probably listening to music. He does that when he can't

112

sleep. I don't want to startle him. I tap gently and slide the door slowly open. He sees me, and he's on his feet instantly, alarmed regardless of my efforts to the contrary, takes the earbuds out, and says, "What is it, Nuha?"

"It's Mama. It's happened again," I reply. "Gigi called. She's done everything by the book. She called Doctor Jareer, and he came over, and Mama is stable. But I need to be there."

"Of course, just give me two minutes. I'm going with you." Khaled leaves me on the balcony and sprints inside. I fill my lungs with the crisp morning air. I remember a time before my 'bad period,' which feels like a millennia ago, when I woke up at four in the morning every day, come rain or shine, hours before anyone in the house stirred. No other time of the day beats those precious hours.

I sit on the chair Khaled just vacated. In his haste, he left behind something tucked under the seat cushion. I suspected this for weeks, and now I have confirmation. I slide my hand under the pillow and bring out the pack of Marlboro Lights. Well, at least he's consistent—still the same brand.

Oh, Khaled! You've been so good for so long. Three whole years! I wish I could help you, *habibi*, but I don't know what to do anymore.

I leave the pack where I found it and lock the balcony door behind me.

2

I have my own key to Big House, but I prefer to knock and let the occupants answer on any other day. However, on this early summer morning, I use my key. The interior is quiet and dark; only a faint light comes from the direction of my mother's room. We follow the light; the door to her room is ajar. I push it quietly and go in. Khaled stands outside and waits. I find my mother on her bed, lying on her back, eyes closed. Gigi is on a chair close by, a mug of something in one hand and her mobile phone in the other. She sees me and turns, and nods her head in an 'all is well' gesture.

My mother is old and frail. Now in her late eighties, she's suffered from hypertension for decades. In the beginning, and many years after, my mother's ailments were well-controlled; she was a model patient and followed all doctors' orders regarding diet and lifestyle. Unfortunately, about two years ago, she developed cardiac arrhythmias, and consequently, eleven months ago had a minor stroke. Despite the medications our family practitioner, after consulting her cardiologist, put her on, we were informed that there would always be a small risk of another stroke. As well as the added chance of her getting fainting spells that could lead to falling and the subsequent fractures in her already osteoporotic bones.

The stroke was transient and left no permanent damage. She was hospitalized then, and after her discharge, I wanted to employ a full-time nurse. My wishes were rejected adamantly. However, her medications and dosages were being altered regularly and had to be supervised. Finally, after a long and serious talk with her, a little cajoling from Khaled, and after consulting our family practitioner, Doctor Jareer, whose personal and professional opinion was that the most important single measure in my mother's management was that she be kept comfortable and stress-free, we reached a compromise. Actually, Gigi was the one who proposed the solution, and we acquiesced.

Gigi, *Allah ykhaliha wa yese'dha*, God bless her, the rock of Big House that she is, suggested that she stay with my mother from now on. She even went further by contacting Doctor Jareer of her own accord to ask him about Mama's medications and what to do if so-or-so scenarios were to transpire. My independent and stubborn mother agreed to Gigi's proposal only because the alternative would be more to her disliking. The negotiations took a while but satisfied everyone in the end.

My mother presented her terms and conditions. My father's half of the bed will stay unoccupied and undisturbed. So, a single bed was squeezed into the empty space between my mother's bedside and the adjacent wall, leaving a narrow lane between the two beds. This necessitated pushing the wardrobe to the far end of the room at a somewhat awkward angle. However, my mother didn't seem to mind the angle, so no one complained.

Another of my mother's stipulations was that she, not Gigi, decides what plays on the TV set in the room. About three years ago, a war erupted between Mama and the Young Aunts about the TV in the sitting room. The hostilities mainly centered on who decided which show to watch and when. To ameliorate the conflict, I suggested that a TV be put up in her bedroom; my mother agreed readily, and to everyone's amusement, the Young Aunts retaliated by setting up their own TV in their bedroom, abandoning the one outside.

And the last of her conditions was that my mother decides when it's lights out, not Gigi. During the time of the talks, I could see the snicker on Gigi's lips and how she tried to hide it, as if she would dream of demanding a channel or turning off the lights and suffering my mother's wrath, so of course, she agreed to all orders but used the momentum of the debate to put in some of her own terms. Firstly, she decides when my mother will take a particular medication, and no arguments are acceptable. She explained that she had everything written down on a timetable, and my mother grunted her assent. Secondly, if she deems it necessary to call the doctor or me, she will, and my mother is not to complain or bicker about it. And finally, regarding her health and well-being, my mother is to listen to Gigi's advice on the matter and not try to contradict her on every issue. I laughed inwardly through these talks, knowing full well that my mother would give Gigi hell, but left it to Gigi's discretion to deal with it as she saw fit.

3

I stand in the bedroom and look at my mother's small body under the covers. I go over to my father's side of the bed, take off my sneakers, and crawl under the blankets. I slink over close to Mama and carefully, so as not to wake her, take her hand into mine. A second passes, then I feel the slightest squeeze on my hand; she's awake. I kiss her forehead, and she responds with a twitch of the lips. I know she's trying to smile. I can see the exhaustion on her features. I whisper close to her ear, "Sleep, Mama. Rest." As if she was waiting for permission, a couple of minutes later, I feel her breathing take on a slower rhythm. I stay close and watch her breathe, look at her features, enjoy the warmth her body is emitting, and inspect every crease and wrinkle on her beautiful face.

I find Khaled and Gigi drinking hot tea in silence. I join them around the table in the middle of the kitchen. Gigi pours me a mug. I wrap my fingers around the hot porcelain and lower my head to smell the minty brew.

"What happened?" I ask and take a sip of my drink.

"Madam got up to use the toilet, and she was very quiet; I didn't wake up," replies Gigi in her heavily accented English. "I always tell her 'wake me up anytime,' but she is stubborn, your mother!" I hear the anxiety in Gigi's voice. "I woke up on the crash; she fell."

"It's ok, Gigi, we all know, and she knows too, that she has a tendency to faint and fall. She should have wakened you," I say in a calm what-happened-happened voice.

Gigi sighs and continues in frustration, "I ran to the bathroom. She was sitting on the floor, her head resting on the edge of the bathtub. I asked her if she was ok, and she shouted, 'Help me up, Gigi, NOW!'"

I look at Khaled and smile. This wasn't the first time Mama fell after a fainting spell. The last time, Gigi refused to help her up, abiding by doctors' orders, and my mother gave her hell, threatening and swearing bloody murder.

"You know Doc Jareer told us never help Madam up after a fall and always call emergency?" Gigi asks rhetorically.

"Yes, we know," I say.

"I ran to the room, I called 911, and I talked to them in Arabic," she announces with a smile, very proud that she can speak Arabic well enough to explain the emergency. "And I called Doc Jareer. He said that he was on-call and not sleeping and that I was lucky to find him up. Yes, and that he would come soon. He asked if she was in pain, I told him I don't think so, and she's shouting at me to help her up. He asked if I called 911, and I told him yes. He said, 'Sit with Madam and keep talking to her, and don't help her to get up!'"

Gigi sees my mug is empty and refills it. I gesture my head toward my aunts' bedroom. She snickers and says, "The two Fs never woke up! Not even when Madam was screaming that she was going to kill me. She has a very loud voice, your mother."

Khaled giggles and gets to his feet. I follow him with my eyes. He paces a few steps around the kitchen and then returns to the table; he fiddles with the sugar bowl and spoon and takes another turn around the kitchen. He's fidgety and distracted, and something is on his mind, as has been the case for some time now. I focus my thoughts on the matter at hand.

Today, *Allah satar*, God protected her. My beautiful, fragile, and stubborn mother, whose body is that of an old woman but whose head is not convinced yet of the fact, has got to be made to understand, as delicately as possible, that she is not young anymore, and asking for help is not beneath her.

Gigi's voice startles me out of my reverie. "They arrived together, the doc and the ambulance. Doc asked me first thing how her talking is. Can you understand it well? I said yes, and he said that is a good sign. Then they went to her, and Doc Jareer examined her from head to feet; do this, Sarah, and do that, Sarah. Look here and look there, Sarah."

As it turns out, and from what I gathered from Gigi, Doctor

Jareer first ruled out a stroke and then examined her for fractures. When he was reasonably sure that she didn't break any bones, they tried to help her to bed, and she refused obstinately to be carried, demanding instead to walk on her own, which she did.

"But Madam is very tired. She's always tired these days. Even a few steps make her tired, and she has to sit down," Gigi tells me sadly. "She is very tired and stubborn. Doctor Jareer said to tell you to call him this afternoon."

A sleepy and disheveled Aunt Fatima saunters from the direction of her bedroom and finds us sitting in the kitchen. "Good morning, beautiful," Khaled chirps. "And how are you this lovely morning?"

Fatima stands glued to the spot, astonishment on her face. She looks at us with her mouth hanging open and eyes wide. "What... what are you doing? Why...?" she asks, then she shakes her head, brings both hands to the sides of her head, and plucks out earplugs from either ear.

"Aha!! Now that explains a lot!" Khaled says with mock seriousness, and looks first at me and then at Gigi.

4

I leave Khaled with the Young Aunts while the two of them explain to him how their niece Melanie, my Aunt Laila's granddaughter, told them that earplugs helped one sleep better and how since then, they've never slept without them. And how it's so much easier than listening to Sarah and Gigi squabbling half of the night every night.

I go to check on Mama, accompanied by Gigi. She's still sleeping like I left her. The room is dark, and the faint fresh smell of *alsabun alnabulsi*, olive oil soap, my mother's distinctive scent, is in the air. I sit on Gigi's bed and lean closer to Mama's prone figure. I listen to her soft breathing and watch her chest rise and fall. Her face has lost its earlier weariness and now looks peaceful. I see Gigi stand in the doorway, unsure whether to come in or leave us be. I end her hesitation by gesturing for her to come in. She sits beside me and whispers, "Ma'am, it's time for Madam's medicine."

"Let her sleep for a while longer. Another half or even a full hour is not the end of the world," I whisper back. Gigi looks doubtful but doesn't argue.

It's about half past ten in the morning when I start the walk from Big House to The Place. Earlier, Khaled had left Big House to go home for a quick shower and a change of clothes before heading to work. Mama had awakened, was pleased when she registered my presence, argued with Gigi about a particular medication, and rebuffed the breakfast tray Gigi had arranged until I sweet-talked her into having something before taking her morning blood pressure tablets. Then she fell asleep again, watching *Yawm Jadid*[*] on her TV.

I enter the shop at about ten minutes to eleven. Saja is at the register, looking at something on her mobile screen. Then, without raising her head, she says, "You're late."

"Observant as usual," I respond.

I take a look around. I notice two customers, a woman in her late thirties sitting on one of the armchairs, a book in one hand and a coffee cup in the other, and an elderly gentleman around the bestsellers next to the coffee station.

I look to the back, to the children's corner. Two days left until our event. I had persuaded Tea that the event needed catering. In the beginning, she had refused steadfastly. "What! Catering? Are you kidding me, Nuha? Crumbs and sticky hands on everything! Is that what you want?! Who would clean up the mess? NO!"

This wasn't our first event; however, it was the first for children, hence Tea's reluctance, but in the end, she relented.

---

[*] Yawm Jadid: (literally) New Day, is a family morning TV program broadcasted daily on Jordan Television.

She knew that hosting such events would benefit our small enterprise, and if we were to proceed with them, we needed to ensure they were executed flawlessly. So when I called Mai, our caterer, I explained the children's situation and that we needed as little sticky and crumbly food as possible; she laughed and said she'd do her best.

I head for my desk. I avoid looking at the bouquet on the coffee table in the middle of the shop. I call Mai to confirm the date and time. All as prearranged. I sit back in my chair and immediately notice the woman put the book on the table and look intently at the bouquet. I see her move her hand toward a flower in the arrangement and touch it. 'Don't touch! Mine!' I mentally admonish. The fierceness of my emotional reaction surprises me more than anything else.

I get up from my chair and move toward the middle of the room, still trying to decide what I intend to do. Maybe I can come up with a reason to move the bouquet. However, both the woman and I are startled by the jingling of the door and the arrival of Tea. Today, she is dressed from head to foot in nothing but bright yellow, very much resembling a ripe banana.

5

I rescue my bouquet. It now perches on my desk next to my computer. It is in a more official location away from preying hands.

The first thing Tea notices is my attire. "You are duller than usual, *azizati*."

"I've been up since four and in Big House," I say and look down at my battered sneakers, jeans, and plain white T-shirt.

"Is it Sarah? Is she ok?" Tea asks with alarm.

I nod my head twice in the affirmative.

"She fell down again, didn't she?" she asks, and before she

hears any of the specifics, she adds, "That stubborn mule!" Turns and walks to the back office.

I follow in step with the swaying banana to her office, thinking I should be offended by her calling my mother a mule, but who am I kidding? My mother is more stubborn than a mule! Today's scenario was no different from the one before; my mother fell because she wouldn't ask for help and her insistence that she could do everything alone and that she's not a baby. I dread the talk that she and I will have this evening. It's not a conversation I relish or haven't had before. I'll think about it later.

"Tea, I'll be spending more time at Big House, and I might be spending less time here. I just thought you should know," I say.

"Of course," she says plainly. "I'll pass by for a visit tomorrow. I should talk some sense into that woman. Today, I have Sadeen's baby shower. You know, Sadeen? Sumaya's daughter." Then, as if it just dawns on her, she enthusiastically adds, "Why don't you come? Areej will be there."

Seriously! Sometimes I feel Tea identifies with me more than anyone else, besides Khaled, that is. And other times, like now, I feel she has no idea. For example, when has she ever seen me in any social gathering, aside from events at The Place? Be that a baby shower, wedding, engagement, or any celebration of any kind? And she's asking me today of all days!

"Come on, we'll have fun. I'm dying to see Sumaya's freshly landscaped garden," she pleads.

I look into her face and find, to my amusement, that she is expectant and waiting for an answer. "No," I respond simply.

"Oh well. Never mind, I just thought..." She trails off. Clearly crestfallen.

"No," I repeat.

Finally, she falls silent. My phone, in the back pocket of my jeans, vibrates once and then falls silent. A message. I know instinctively who it's from. I am so confident of this knowledge that I don't even get my phone out to make sure.

"All is a go for Thursday," I tell Tea. "I'll be here bright and early on the day, but I might not come tomorrow. I love you, Tea. Have fun this evening." Then I turn and leave her office.

Once outside, I get my phone out, unlock it, open WhatsApp, and read the message.

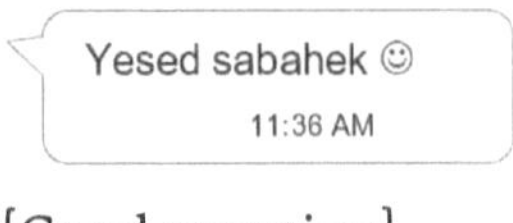

[Good morning]

The fifth message from him joins those above it—all unanswered. But unbeknownst to the sender, eagerly anticipated.

Saturday 17 sep.

I asked mommy today. Why is it called the red sea?
She thought and thought and thought and then siad
that she didn't know why its called the red sea,
its just a name. Mommy then laughed and siad the
dead sea is easier, it is called dead because nothing
lives inside it. There are no fishes or anything!

I asked my mommy if we can go to the dead sea
if we don't go to the red sea? And she siad why
don't you want to go to the red sea? and I siad
that I DO want to go the the red sea but that I
am afraid M will not get good grades because he is
stupid. Mommy then was very cross with me and
siad: Faten you should not call anyone stupid and
M is not stupid. And we should never call people
names.

And then she left my room ☹

The best thing that happened to me today:
Nothing ☹

I love my mommy so much. She is the pretiest mommy in the world.

Dear diary do you think I should apologise?

CHAPTER 12

1

I stand in my bedroom and scrutinize what I see in the full-length mirror. Skin still wet from the shower, damp hair falls lifeless around my scrubbed face and touches my shoulders. I try to stand up straighter, and I try to smile. The smile doesn't touch my eyes; I try to make it reach my eyes, but fail. Then my eyes catch the dress on the armchair in the corner.

No messages yesterday. Did he finally comprehend that I was not interested? Was I interested? I dreamed of him last night. Dreaming of him might not be the correct depiction. I felt him last night. I thought of him last night. I study my reflection again. My index finger trails down the side of my neck, slowly over my shoulder, traces the collarbone back to the center into the shallow indentation between the two clavicles, down the valley between my breasts, and lingers there momentarily. Then continues following the top lace of my bra over my right breast and then down my side, gently to the dip of my waist, lower still until it rests over my hip. I look deep into the reflection of my eyes. I want to look desirable. That thought materializes in my conscious mind without warning. It feels imperative that I do so. My eyes leave their reflection and go back to look at the armchair in the corner.

The hem stops just above the knee, formfitting at the waist and around the hips, with a flared skirt. Sleeveless with a high, round neckline and made with silky, flowy material of the brightest red. I gaze into the mirror. I look into the eyes of the stranger standing in front of me. A week ago, something shifted, and a longing inside me stirred. Before, and for many years, this stranger was everything that I tried never to be.

2

I venture into the kitchen. Khaled serves scrambled eggs on two plates; toast and orange juice are already on the counter. He has his back to me; he doesn't see me come in but hears me.

"Take a seat, beautiful. I'll pour the tea in a minute," he says.

I watch Khaled walk to the sink; his back is still to me. He rinses the pan and then turns to face me.

Khaled was never a person of hasty responses. On the contrary, for as long as I've known him, he possessed the mellowest temperament. Always sedate on the uptake, never quick in condemning a person or judging a situation. He sees me in my new red dress. We have been married for four years, and the expression on his face now is unique. I can't interpret the emotion behind it, a combination of love and melancholy maybe, but chiefly concern. He looks at me and tilts his head to the right, then to the left, as if the change in the angle might change the perspective. I nonchalantly take a sip of orange juice. He says nothing but breaks the stare and starts to pour the tea.

Khaled has been my best friend long before becoming my husband. We have been together for decades; I'd seen him at his strongest and his weakest. He'd seen me at my darkest. He's no longer just a friend or a partner. A correct depiction would be my rock and campus. Our recent communication failure is not because we don't know each other well enough. In fact, it's quite the opposite, because we know each other too well.

I wait for him to say something. I need him to tell me what to do. I needn't ask for his help because it will come regardless—if not today, then soon. I wait. He looks into my eyes again. I sip my hot tea and eat a forkful of my eggs, never breaking eye contact. We are sharing an eloquent soundless conversation, not a defiant one. Then finally—it must be the earnest expression on my face—he speaks. He knows that whatever words he chooses, he will find a sincere listener in me. But of all the things he can say and the lectures he can give, he picks two words. "Be careful."

3

I pass by Big House on my way to work. Gigi opens the door for me; she tells me that my mother is still asleep and assures me they had an uneventful night. I follow her to the kitchen, where I find Feryal and Fatima already up and having their morning cups of Turkish coffee. My Young Aunts are avid coffee drinkers, and having coffee is more a ceremonial affair for them than merely drinking a beverage. So, when Gigi offers to make me a cup, I notice that Feryal gets up and walks to the stove. "Go check on Sarah; I'll make the coffee," she tells Gigi.

"Making coffee is an art," she starts, addressing me, and I straighten up in my seat, ready to listen to the sermon I have heard many times before. "It's not just dissolving ground coffee into hot water. It's so much more." My Aunt Feryal falls silent, and Aunt Fatima, who is sitting next to me, picks up where her twin left off, "You have to have the right mindset for brewing it."

A steaming coffee cup is in front of me; I take a whiff of the tantalizing aroma. I believe coffee smells so much better than it actually tastes, a belief that my aunts decidedly disregarded when I expressed it in the past. Today, however, I stay silent as I don't want to distract them from the real reason they wished Gigi out of the kitchen.

"So," Fatima starts as a prelude for the highly anticipated topic. "Nice dress."

"Very becoming on you," adds Feryal.

"Can't remember the last time I saw you in a dress. When was it?" Fatima questions.

"*Kateb ketabha*[*] four years ago," Feryal answers Fatima. "What's the occasion?" Feryal inquires.

"Very nice. Why don't you do it more often?" Fatima probes.

"Today, we have a literary event in The Place," I simply answer them. As if this is how I always dress for such events.

"Which reminds me, when do you want us to be there?" Fatima asks.

I silently groan.

"There where?" I ask, feigning innocence. I need time to think of a way to dissuade them.

"Madam T will be distraught if we're not there," Fatima declares and looks at Feryal, who nods her agreement.

'No, she really, really won't!' I think, but don't dare say. I try not to sound too fervent when I speak, "But it's a children's event, Aunties. You'll be very bored."

This makes them laugh in unison. "We are always bored in your shop, *habibti*," Fatima says.

Then, Feryal announces, "There's nothing to do there except drink bad coffee. But we don't want to upset Madam T."

4

Despite my excursion, I still arrive at The Place before anyone else. I open up and turn the coffee machine on. I carry one of the extra folding tables from the back and set it up next to the coffee station where Mai will arrange the food she's serving today. I head to my desk and sit down. The flowers are starting to wilt but can survive another few days. I caress one of the petals gingerly. Bend down and smell one of the white roses. I hear the faint vibration inside my bag. Again, I know this message is from him before I get the phone out. Did he sense that I just admired his gift?!

---

[*] Kateb Alketab: The Islamic religious ceremony in which a marriage contract is signed.

There are two types of elation. The first is the happiness you feel when you reach a goal, win a prize, or watch a loved one succeed. And then, there is the other kind of elation. The all-consuming type. The earth-shattering type. The bliss that makes your heart stutter just thinking about the possibilities before they happen. This is a mystical experience that transcends any previous sorrow, no matter how deep the pain.

The ecstasy that I feel right now is of the second category. Over the last week, the change that has come over me is quite staggering in its magnitude, and I find myself reeling. I don't know how to stop it or slow it down, or even if I want to do either.

I open my phone and go to my WhatsApp messages. I notice Zaid has changed his profile picture. I tap on it, and it expands; his eyes bore into mine. Another selfie, but no smile, just a brooding look. No sunglasses this time, instead black, intense eyes. Facial hair is longer in this photo, less neat than in its predecessor. I read the most recent messages.

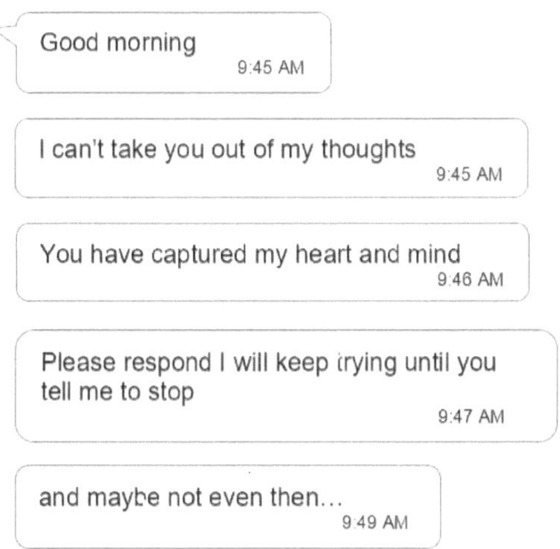

He was voicing my thoughts. I, too, can't take him out of my thoughts. He, too, has captured my mind, and my heart (had I had one). I want to respond but don't know how to do it. I want to but can't. How can I? What if I do, and he wants to get to know me better? What if he really gets to know how broken I am?

I look into the distance as if in a trance. Through the window, I stare at the tree on the opposite side of the road. I notice a car pass by. I watch a taxi stop and drop off a woman carrying two shopping bags, one in each hand. I watch two teenage girls stop in front of the ice cream shop. A delivery van idles past and disappears around the corner. I look at my flowers. I stand up and look more intently at the red lilies. Finally, I pluck out one of them.

Since owning a smartphone and using WhatsApp, I've always kept the default blank profile image. Now, I am studying my newly uploaded profile photo. It is a selfie I just took five minutes ago. My face looking into the camera, devoid of any makeup but for mascara, shows a hint of a smile. My wavy golden-brown hair is loose, parted in the middle, and touches my red-swathed shoulders. One red lily nestles in my hair behind one ear.

Ten minutes have passed since I uploaded my non-verbal reply to him. I sit on the Chesterfield and look attentively at my phone in front of me on the coffee table. It vibrates. I take a deep breath.

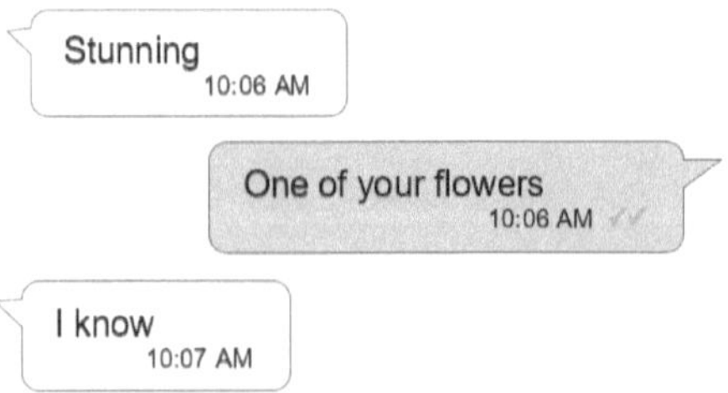

I have no more to say for now. I close my phone. He seems to understand. He, too, says no more.

5

Saja comes in at about half past ten. She is in a green sundress with gold strappy sandals. She looks striking. Her smile is spread from ear to ear, and her step has a definite bounce. Then she spots me, and this somewhat dampens her sunny disposition. "You're early," she says.

"Good morning. Actually, I came in later than usual. Busy day today," I retort.

"Uh-huh," she responds dismissively.

"You look gorgeous," I venture, trying to get on her good side for today. No need for a sulky Saja if I can prevent it.

"Nice dress!" she snaps back.

Of course, I know what's wrong with her. I've known for a week. But acknowledging it will generate consequences I am not ready to deal with now. So I ignore her sharp reaction and say, "Thank you. I don't usually..."

"No! You don't usually, do you?" she snaps, cutting me off mid-sentence, more irritable than before, and disappears to the back room. Where, with any luck, she will spend a significant amount of time.

The queen of color makes her entrance at eleven o'clock sharp and puts my red dress and Saja's green one to shame. Tea dons a knee-length shimmery bronze sequined dress with long puffy chiffon sleeves, figure-hugging with a plunging V-shaped neckline showing a considerable part of her ample bosom. But what makes the ensemble particularly striking isn't the dress as much as the footwear. Tea has on black army boots with gold buckles and studs. Tea works this way; her energy, air, and confidence are magic. Just by looking at her, I know this day will be a success.

Saja comes out when she hears the jingling announcing Tea's arrival. Tea doesn't disappoint with her enthusiasm when she sees us. She claps her hands together in a gesture of admiration. "Oh! Look at you both. *Btjanenu!*"

"Look at YOU!" I say in awe. "Tea, you have outdone your-self."

Not one for false modesty, Tea assertively says, "Yes, I know. And it cost a pretty penny too."

Saja is back to whatever she is doing. Tea and I sit opposite each other in the center of the room. She looks at me intently. I initially thought she would admire me, ooh and aah, make me twirl, and make a big deal of my appearance. However, it seems that the opening praise was the only one I am get-ting today. Tea regards me with a worried stare. The concern I hear in her words somehow irritates me beyond measure. "So, what's new, *habibti*? What have you been up to lately?"

"It's like I can't win with you!" I snap at her. Tea visibly flinches. "What do you want from me? How, in your opinion, should I live my fucked-up life, Tea? Huh?"

"Nuha *habibti*, I didn't mean it like that," she responds sin-cerely.

"You look too dull, Nuha!" I try to imitate her voice and use words she's used before. "What?! I'm too bright for you now?" Even while uttering the words, I know I am completely off the mark and crossing a line, but I say them anyway.

"That is not what I meant, and you know it!" Her voice is several octaves higher. Tea can always give as good as she gets. "Save it. I'm not in the mood for belligerent Nuha today. No, thank you very much!" She stands abruptly and leaves me seething.

My mind reels, trying to fathom my foul mood. I stand up and walk purposefully to the children's corner. I look for something to do. Books are in neat stacks. Shelves and sur-faces are clean and shiny. I try desperately to find anything to occupy my hands to give me time to try and make sense of my outburst.

And just as I am about to give up, I see it on the top shelf two rows from where I am standing: a children's storybook with a dandelion on the cover. It is so clear now; the image my mind summons is so incredibly sharp it blinds me. I sit down on one of the small beanbags, my heart racing inside my chest. I start to rock back and forth. This is how Tea finds me a few minutes later, rocking back and forth. She puts her hand on my shoulder and squeezes.

"It's ok, *habibti*. It's ok," she says softly.

"No, it's not, Tea. It really is not," I respond with desperation.

"Tell me," she whispers close to my ear.

Silence. A minute passes. Her hand is still on my shoulder.

I stagger up off the beanbag. "You know what, Tea? Today is not about me; it's about Jamila. Let's make this work," I say, then I hug her tightly to me. "I'm sorry for the way I acted." I walk off in the direction of the restrooms. She says something, but I don't catch it.

6

Jamila, a mother of five and still in her early thirties, is a gifted bilingual writer. Her first book, *Rasha and the Rainbowfish*, was followed in succession by *Masa and her Mischievous Monkey* and *Maysa and the Morning Moon*. Rasha, Masa, and Maysa are the names of Jamila's three eldest daughters. The books were a success, and we continuously order new copies. Her fourth book, *Fuad Alfannan* (Fuad the Artist), was written in Arabic and portrayed her fourth child and eldest son, Fuad. Today, we will launch her fifth children's book, named after her youngest son Faris, also in Arabic, *Faris Alfaris* (Faris the Knight).

Jamila and her five children are the first to arrive at The Place almost forty-five minutes before the event is scheduled to commence. We hug, and I kiss her cheeks and the cheeks of all the kids. The shop is almost empty but for two regular customers, a middle-aged couple I see here often perusing the bestsellers. The children see the beanbags at the back and race toward them. Jamila and I follow in their direction, and I hear their mother warn that when people come in, they must get up and give the beanbags to customers to sit on. Cries, protests, and statements like "It's not fair" and "Why, Mama?" follow this announcement. Faris especially is downcast and says with tears about to spill from his eyes, "But, Mama! The book is mine, my name, it's about me!"

"He does have a point," I hear Tea shout from the back room.

Addressing her youngest, Jamila says, "How about..." stops, thinks for a minute, and then continues, "you sit on my lap on the big beanbag chair while I'm reading your story?" This suggestion seems to sit well with Faris because he saunters off toward the big beanbag, and to his older siblings' chagrin, climbs on and sits there as if reserving the spot.

Mai and her culinary wares are next to come in through the main entrance. With Saja's help and several trips to her van, the goods are spread on the table designated for the purpose. Jamila's children receive one cookie each that Mai assures will not crumble excessively and are told to please try to avoid making a mess. Tea comes out from her office and is livid, eyeing me with an I-told-you-so look.

"I don't know how you manage, *Um Fuad*," Tea says, addressing Jamila. "If it were me, they would have locked me up by now."

Jamila sits on the Chesterfield opposite us. She wears a neat dark gray pantsuit; her hair is covered with a light cream-colored hijab, and she has a pretty face with an incredibly clear complexion. Despite having had five children in a short time, her figure is clearly athletic looking. I know for a fact that her star is rising in literary circles, and she's starting to become a household name, at least in households where children roam.

Jamila squares up to answer Tea, but then she sees the look on my face, which visibly states, 'Don't bother,' and falls silent.

"So, what's your next project now that you have five books

named after your five children?" I interject.

"Don't tell me you're planning on having a sixth child?" Tea cackles.

"No, five is just the right number *Alhamdulillah*," Jamila laughs aloud. "I'm thinking of one with all of them in it."

Just then, the door jingles, announcing the first of our guests. I see the Young Aunts cross the threshold, the strain from the walk evident on their wrinkled faces. Tea looks at me in wonder, her expression openly communicating, 'What are they doing here?'

"I didn't invite them, if that's what you're thinking," I say.

"Then why did they come?" she asks, bewildered.

"Because, my dear Tea, they think you'd be very upset if they didn't." I chuckle, making my way to welcome the twins.

7

We have a good turnout; I count twenty-five youngsters and eight adults. The small beanbags are holding two children each. The rest are cross-legged on the carpets. The adults stand, forming a semicircle around the children's corner. Jamila is reading, and all are listening intently, children as well as adults.

I smell Zaid before I see him. I recall Tea inviting him verbally when he personally delivered the beanbag chairs. Still, I don't think he would have come had I not sent him my own private invitation in the form of my WhatsApp profile picture with a lily in my hair. I stand facing the assembled crowd with my back to him. I feel his presence fill The Place. In my peripheral vision, Saja darts past me. I hear Tea's voice welcoming him and making introductions. I don't move or make a sound. For all intents and purposes, I am engrossed in the story being read. Yet, in reality, a volcano is erupting within me. I hear my name being called, albeit in a hushed voice, so as not to disrupt the ongoing function.

I can't make sense of why I feel it's necessary to appear absorbed in the activities. Still, eventually, I turn slowly and feign surprise at the view that meets me. I think everyone believes my performance, bar the person it was meant for—Zaid himself. He meets my gaze with an amused look and a lopsided smile. I take a few steps toward the middle of the room, and to my amazement, I find that my Young Aunts are already on a first-name basis with him.

"Zaid, this is our niece, Nuha," Feryal says, making the introduction.

I hear a low scoff from the register where Saja perches, and I ignore it.

Zaid gets up from his seat and extends his hand toward me. "*Tsharafna sitti*, pleased to meet you."

His hand squeezes mine ever so slightly, and I withdraw it quickly. "A pleasure," I reply.

"Nuha owns half of this place, and this place is called The Place," Fatima says in amusement, and both aunts collapse in a fit of laughter as if this is the funniest thing in the world.

"It's a very nice place," he tells me politely.

"Thank you," I say, looking into his eyes.

"Absolutely exquisite," he adds.

"Thank you," I repeat.

"Breathtaking," he whispers so only I can hear. However, Saja, the lip reader at the register, jumps off her stool and storms to the back office.

"What is wrong with that girl?" Tea asks no one in particular. "She's been in a huff all day. And I haven't seen her take one photo for our socials like I asked!"

I excuse myself and return to Jamila and the reading that just concluded. I hear a buzz of activity, and someone asks Jamila to read another one of her stories. She agrees, and I go to one of the shelves to retrieve *Masa and her Mischievous Monkey*. After handing the book to Jamila, I turn and find Zaid standing right next to me.

"Can we talk for a minute, if you please?" he politely asks.

"Talk? About what? What do we have to talk about?" I answer his question with a barrage of my own.

He ignores the brusque tone, replying with, "There are so many things I want to say to you. Give me a chance."

I feel it looking at me; I look up at it. The dandelion leers back at me. Taunting me from its location on the shelf.

"I'm so sorry," I tell him. I shake my head, trying to clear my mind. "Please! Leave."

Clearly taken aback, he takes a step away from me.

8

Khaled is on the balcony when I get home. "How did it go?" he asks expectantly.

"Great. All ran smoothly, and the sales were better than we expected. Oh yes, and there is a big stain on the carpet that Tea still doesn't know about."

Khaled laughs wholeheartedly.

I leave him, professing exhaustion after a long day, and flee to the bedroom. I go about my nighttime routine methodically and in quick succession. I turn my bedside lamp on and turn off the main light switch. I sit on my bed. I look at my nightstand. I pick up the first of the framed photographs and kiss it. I pick up the other and do the same. I get under the covers and pick up the notebook with the dandelion. I hold it to my chest and hug it closely. "I promise you, never again. You are my number one. I promise I promise I promise..." I repeat over and over, rocking back and forth. In my haste to look desirable and pretty this morning, I forgot my morning routine. I promise I will never forget it again. I put the notebook back where I found it. I switch off the light. I wait for sleep to come.

9

Sleep doesn't come. At three in the morning, I sit up in bed. I compose, delete, and recompose. I send one text message.

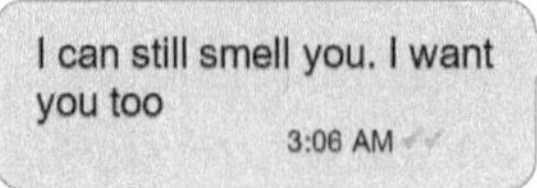

sunday 18 sep.

when mommy came into my room today. She wasn't cross any more but I siad I'm sorry to her and she siad why? what did you do? And I siad because I siad M is stupid and she laughed and siad that she loved me and she loved M and she loved daddy too and that we should not call each other bad names. I siad I promise not to say it any more and she hugged me.

Taesar will also come with us to the red sea. Daddy siad this and I am ~~iksited~~ excited about that.

The best thing that happened to me today.

1. Mommy is not cross with me and she still loves me

2. I went to M's room and I asked him if he's studying to get good grades so that we can go to the red sea. He siad yes he is and I siad show me your science homwork to make sure you know it and he siad to me it is not your business Faten.

But I ~~insestet~~ insisted that he show me so he did and it was good. (I think that grade 2 is so much easier that grade 3) So dear diary there is hope ☺

3. Taesar + red sea = FUN!

Good night

CHAPTER 13

1

He came into my life and established himself in it. He's now a constant, a steady presence. He's with me all the time; if not in person, he resides in my thoughts. When he's away, I miss him, long for him, and ache for his touch. When he's near, I savor his proximity and lose myself in his solidity and strength, both physically and emotionally.

I lie next to my sleeping mother, who has been asking for my company more than usual in recent days. Tonight, in the early morning hours, sleep abandons me. I stare into the darkness and listen to her breathing. A smile creeps to my lips when I think of him, and I feel little tendrils of happiness engulf me. Moments like this one have become my favorite throughout the day, when only thoughts of him surface.

Some nights, I wrap myself in thoughts of him and slowly drift into a sound sleep. Other nights, like tonight, are more challenging. The need is fiercer; I long for him, and the fantasy alone is not enough. Still, my eyes gaze into the darkness, and my hands roam over my belly, contemplating what his hands would do. What would his caress be like? Will his fingers be gentle? Like they sometimes are. Or will they torment me and be demanding and authoritative? Like I prefer.

What am I doing?!

I jump out of bed as quickly and quietly as I can, considering the craziness that seized me seconds ago. I leave the room, keep the door wide open, and pad barefoot to the kitchen. I find Gigi drinking some hot beverage and noiselessly giggling at something displayed on her mobile screen. She raises her head when she hears me enter.

"Cannot sleep, ma'am?" she asks with a smile still on her face.

"I woke up an hour ago and couldn't go back to sleep," I answer. "You're up early. What time is it?" I raise my wrist to discover that I must have left my watch on the edge of the bathroom sink.

"It's three in the morning here, but in Manila, it is nine in the morning. The daughter of my dead father's dead sister had a baby boy yesterday."

"Congratulations, Gigi. You can say your cousin had a baby. It's much easier," I tease and head for the electric kettle to turn it on.

"Want me to make you tea?" she asks and stands abruptly.

"No, no. I'll do it, but keep an ear out for Mama in case she wakes up."

She sits back down tentatively and studies the tablecloth. Something is clearly on her mind. I hasten to reduce her unease and ask, "Is something wrong, Gigi?"

"Nothing wrong, no, ma'am. But will you stay every night in Big House now?"

The panic that grabs me is almost imperceptible. Gigi doesn't notice; it needs someone more attuned to me to detect it. Khaled would have sensed it. I cannot handle any changes disrupting my established night and morning routines. Not now, on top of all the changes I have allowed recently. If Mama needs me, of course. If there is no other way, then by all means, but if there is no need, I cannot handle any more changes now. Finally, I get ahold of my wits and answer as calmly as possible, "No, I don't think that's necessary. You're doing a great job with her. Just when she asks me to stay, I will."

Something still irks me; even after responding to her inquiry, I'm still flustered. As if my point has yet to go through, I need to say more to nail it in. "You do know what I mean, right?" I ask firmly.

"Yes, ok, ma'am," she replies.

2

My 'bad period' isn't over; I am endlessly incarcerated within its web. However, I know how to control the fear now; I teeter on the brink, but what prevents me from falling are the rules I laid down for myself. They are my anchor; they ground me, comfort me, make me feel in control. If I venture out of my comfort zone, it is always a controlled experiment. I now dare to wander off my path, but I hate being questioned about it or called on it.

In the past, any word or query from anyone directed at my established routines, regardless of how innocent they may be, generated an agitation in me that sometimes bordered on a full-scale panic attack. Years have passed since such an episode occurred, but nowadays, if I sense that my ways are being challenged, remnants of the old discomfort surface.

I finish my tea, and it is still dark outside. I walk back to Mama's room, and she is as I left her—sound asleep. I sit on my father's side of the bed and gaze at his nightstand, unchanged since his passing. The illumination from the hallway, always kept on at night, is enough to discern the two framed photographs standing side by side. They are two girls of approximately the same age, eleven or thereabout. One is a black-and-white photo, and the other is a colored one. The two girls resemble each other to a great extent. The photos were taken decades apart; the monochrome is of my long-dead half-sister, and the other is of me.

On my father's nightstand, objects came and went for as long as I can remember—books, reading glasses, a transistor radio, and an assortment of medication bottles—but the two constants were the frames. The photo of my half-sister has always stayed the same. On the other hand, the one of me altered four or five times as I grew up until I reached eleven. I never understood why he never changed it after that. I asked him once when I was about fifteen if he'd like to take a new photo of me to replace the old one on his nightstand. I recall he was very diplomatic in his justification to me on that occasion. He hugged me and told me that he loved me and loved all my pictures, whatever my age was in them. A few days later, he took new photos of Mama and me and had them developed. One, in particular, was blown up, framed, and placed on the living room's corner table, but the one on the nightstand stayed the same. The years have taught me to never question the logic behind the actions of someone who is grieving.

3

I'm in The Place looking through last week's accounts, and Tea is in the back doing what Tea usually does in the back. Saja is sulking at the register. I'm considering discussing her attitude and having it out with her. Tea has recently, on more than one occasion, commented on Saja's newly adopted petulant disposition, and regardless of the underlying foundation for her sullenness, which I can guess at, we have a business to run, and Saja's attitude is not doing miracles in attracting customers.

On my way from my desk to the register, the phone vibrates in my pocket. My insides turn into a molten mess when I see 'Zaid' on the screen, which ultimately defers the intended confrontation to a future date. All other worries are pushed aside, and I can only think about seeing him tonight.

I know three facts: the first, Zaid is infatuated with me or the idea of me; it's difficult to discern which. The second, Zaid doesn't register a person in my life named Khaled. The third fact is that, regardless of his sentiments toward me and the reasons behind them, I need him in my life more than he realizes.

I tried to resist. I tried to treat his appearance in my life as inconsequential. I tried to discourage his onslaught and reduce his eagerness. My efforts, however, did not fare well and rapidly deteriorated, and in no time after our acquaintance started, Zaid became besotted with me. In the beginning, it was such that I thought he was joking. He, however, found no humor when I often laughed at his impetuous nature. Elaborate bouquets were delivered to The Place almost daily until I asked him to cease and desist, and even then, I didn't feel he took me seriously. Then, poetic love verses flooded my inboxes, in addition to the flowers, which now are delivered weekly after my insistence that they stop altogether. Zaid idolizes me, but he doesn't really know me. He has a vision of me that he worships, but he doesn't see the real me.

I myself am obsessed with Zaid, and there is no reason to deny it. My life now is ingrained with his and his with mine. And yet, one thought rankles me; I've never kept that I'm married a secret, yet Zaid ignores this fact. Ours is an illicit affair to any bystander, yet he never asks me about Khaled or refers to him by name or context. This point does not sit well with me, so the other day, I purposefully brought up the subject of Khaled. Initially, it was as if he didn't hear me. We were at his place, and I had just got in, and he was cooking for me. I sat and looked at him; I knew he'd heard me, and I waited. Finally, he lowered the heat on whatever was simmering on the stove, came over, sat on the chair next to me, edged the chair closer to mine, and awkwardly took me into his arms. "Please don't leave me," he said into my hair. And that was all he had for me on that subject.

I soon discovered that it wasn't that he didn't pay heed to Khaled; instead, he feared the threat he thought Khaled posed. Zaid is jealous of Khaled, and I suspect he believes that one day I might regret what I have with him and go back to my husband, which is another untruth that Zaid's infatuated mind has fabricated. He needs to understand that what we share has nothing to do with Khaled. And that I haven't left Khaled, nor do I intend to do so. I feel that Zaid has envisioned that we will be together sooner or later and that it's just a matter of time until he convinces me. My suspicions arise from what he says and how he acts, none suggesting that he thinks what's between us is temporary. It isn't an ideal way to deal with life, but I am not the best judge of how people should lead their lives. I grasp his reasoning, albeit flawed, and am flattered by it. I promise myself that when the time comes, and I have to tell him my truth, I will explain everything. But for now, and as long as possible, I want things to remain unchanged.

I answer his call.

"*Omri*," he says. His greeting to me whenever he hears my voice: My life.

4

Tea, who has an opinion on everything, said nothing when she witnessed the bouquets of flowers appear at our doorstep every day. She offered no comments on my recent preoccupations, or on my recent out-of-character bouts of unexpected laughter, or the adolescent blushes that surface on my cheeks whenever a message beeps on my phone.

Today, she finds me giggling on the phone with Zaid. I am sitting cross-legged on the beanbag at the back of the store. I see her expression, and I intuit that today is the day that Tea decides to break the silence. I am glad and ready; I want to have it out with her and be done with it. Tea is my friend and, for lack of a better description, my savior, or at least one of them. I end the phone call with a promise to see him later.

"Nuha *habibti*, I love you, and all that, and I just wanted to..."

"I want this, Tea. I need this! I need him," I cut her off short. "So, whatever you think you need to tell me, keep in mind that for now, at least, he's good for me. Is there anything else you need to say?" I ask. The expression 'best defense is a good offense' applies here. I know I don't need to defend myself to Tea, but time has taught me that being upfront with her is always easier.

"You should..." she says in response to my gush, then stops. "Of course, if that's what you want..." She stops for a few seconds as if regaining her footing and tries again, "But I was thinking of later, not now, *hayati*. Maybe..."

"Maybe what?" I ask her. I'm on my feet, facing her now. "What is there to think about, Tea?" There is pleading in my voice. "It's an impossible situation, Tea, whichever way you look at it."

Surprised by my intensity, she falls silent again to consider what to say next. But really, what was she expecting? Me sitting down with her and discussing slowly and rationally the pros and cons of having an affair? And yet, I owe her more than that. I take a deep breath and continue, "Tea, I know you are worried about me. I understand. And I know the reality that it will have to end eventually. But that aside, I need this now. It's been so long that I've needed anything as much. Please try to grasp my twisted reasoning. Can you do that for me?"

I sympathize with Tea; she is a person with a positive outlook on every situation, and an opinion on every topic, except when it comes to me. I know she loves and watches out for me, but I have never made it easy for her. She dives headfirst into arguments and relishes it. Still, with me, she always staggers and stops, not wanting to hurt me, and I am ashamed to say I take full advantage of this fact, but unbeknownst to her, I love her all the more for it.

"I just don't want to see you hurt," she tells me.

"Hurt," I repeat the word as if it is foreign. "Hurt," I repeat blandly. "Really?!" I question solemnly. "Tea, if anyone is going to get hurt in this, it won't be me."

Tea busies herself with something mundane, and then I

see her flirting with a customer in her usual boisterous manner. I understand the issue is still unresolved, and we haven't discussed anything substantial yet. Nevertheless, it's good that the topic is now out in the open. At this point, I feel like I can act on my own accord in front of her. She had her chance to share her thoughts and talk to me, but she faltered. In times like these, I hate the 'broken me,' that part of me that makes the people I love, and who I know to love me back, suffer needlessly.

5

Zaid's place is a fifteen-minute drive from The Place. I get there, and he's holding the door open for me. I step in, and his lips accost mine. This time, like every time before it, something inside me clinches with desire. Nothing in my dreams—and I had dreamed of his lips before I felt them on mine—could have prepared me for the real thing. The way he moves slowly toward me, eyes gazing right into mine and seizing my lips with his, takes my breath away. The way he explores my mouth is exquisite. His taste and smell are delicious; the longer we linger, the more I want. Finally, a low, husky moan escapes me, and he stops.

"Tell me what you're thinking?" he murmurs in my ear.

"Don't stop," I whisper back with a sigh.

"I cooked for you; don't you want to eat?"

"No!"

He kisses my neck and inhales. "I love your smell."

With a deep sigh, he pulls me closer, and his mouth retakes mine. His hands hold my back and pull me to him. I push up and wrap my legs around his waist. His teeth gently bite my lower lip, then his warm tongue traces the place where his teeth made contact. It goes on like this, his teeth biting and his tongue soothing the sting of the bite.

I'm lost in such an excruciating ache that I only realize I'm in his bedroom when he places me on the edge of the bed. "Tell me what you're thinking?" he whispers again into my ear.

"Not on the bed," I tell him, looking deep into his scorching black eyes. I point to the wall behind him. "Right there, right now, Zaid. Please!"

"*Omri*," he whispers. He picks me up again, and my legs go back around him.

Minutes later, he inhales deeply, and when he exhales, a silent scream escapes my lips when I instinctively arch in abandon to meet him and meet the sudden pain and immense pleasure. He pushes me against the wall, my legs encircle him, my hands are buried in his hair, every muscle tightens around him, and I close my eyes in surrender. I want to stop breathing, as if breathing might distract me from this exquisite feeling.

"Open your eyes, baby." His throaty voice enters my senses. "I want to look into your eyes. I want to see."

Obediently, I do. My eyes meet the inferno of his gaze, which only intensifies the burning desire where our bodies unite. And just before I feel the abyss of pure pleasure about to engulf me, I remember his words and keep my eyes open and locked onto his, so he can see.

6

I'm home. I didn't eat at Zaid's, and I didn't stay a while longer like he wanted me to. He was upset, and I didn't like that I upset him. Today, I fell asleep in his arms, only to wake an hour later to my preset phone alarm, and I jumped out of bed as if it caught fire. He knows I would never stay the night, and I'm sure he doesn't expect me to. Still, contrary to what I think he thinks the reason is, my motivation has nothing to do with my marital status. The reality is that the longer I'm away, the stronger my urge becomes to be grounded in my sanctuary, rituals, and calm. I will try to make him understand someday, but today was not the day.

Khaled isn't home. He had called and told me that he was staying out late tonight. I have to talk to him soon and tell him what's been going on in my life; there are many things we both need to say and many things to discuss.

I take a shower, and I go about my nighttime routine methodically and in quick succession. I turn my bedside lamp on and turn off the main light switch. I sit on my bed. I look at my nightstand. I take the first photograph and kiss it, and then I take the second and do the same. I hold the spiral notebook with the dandelion and kiss it. I hug it close to my chest and gently rock with it in my arms; I do not read from it tonight and place it back where I found it. Instead, I pick up the plain spiral notebook without a picture on the cover. I get under the covers and sit with my legs crossed. I place the notebook before me and open it to a blank page. I start writing.

I'm sorry I'm sorry I'm sorry I'm sorry I'm sorry I'm sorry
I'm sorry I'm sorry I'm sorry I'm sorry I'm sorry I'm sorry
I'm sorry I'm sorry I'm sorry I'm sorry I'm sorry I'm sorry
I'm sorry I'm sorry I'm sorry I'm sorry I'm sorry I'm sorry
I'm sorry I'm sorry I'm sorry I'm spry I'm sorry I'm sorry
I'm sorry I'm sorry I'm sorry I'm sorry I'm sorry I'm sorry
I'm sorry I'm sorry I'm sorry I'm sorry I'm sorry I'm sorry
I'm sorry I'm sorry I'm sorry I'm sorry I'm sorry I'm sorry
I'm sorry I'm sorry I'm sorry I'm sorry I'm sorry I'm sorry
I'm sorry I'm sorry I'm sorry I'm sorry I'm sorry I'm sorry
I'm sorry I'm sorry I'm sorry I'm sorry I'm sorry I'm sorry
I'm sorry I'm sorry I'm sorry I'm sorry I'm sorry I'm sorry
I'm sorry I'm sorry I'm sorry I'm sorry I'm sorry I'm sorry
I'm sorry I'm sorry I'm sorry I'm sorry I'm sorry I'm sorry
I'm sorry I'm sorry I'm sorry I'm sorry I'm sorry I'm sorry
I'm sorry I'm sorry I'm sorry I'm sorry I'm sorry I'm sorry
I'm sorry I'm sorry I'm sorry I'm sorry I'm sorry I'm sorry
I'm sorry I'm sorry I'm sorry I'm sorry I'm sorry I'm sorry
I'm sorry I'm sorry I'm sorry I'm sorry I'm sorry I'm sorry
I'm sorry I'm sorry I'm sorry I'm sorry I'm sorry I'm sorry
I'm sorry I'm sorry I'm sorry I'm sorry I'm sorry I'm sorry
I'm sorry I'm sorry I'm sorry I'm sorry I'm sorry I'm sorry
I'm sorry I'm sorry I'm sorry I'm sorry I'm sorry I'm sorry
I'm sorry I'm sorry **I AM SORRY!**

CHAPTER 14

1

Khaled looks doubtfully at his phone. "Are you sure?" he asks me.

"I'm quite sure," I answer him confidently. "Surely we can survive a day with our phones off, Khaled. Come on!"

"Can we really do this?" He looks genuinely perplexed. I feel him searching his mind for a way out. "What if Gigi calls?" He regrets asking a split second after the words escape his lips. "I'm sorry, I just meant in case... You know? *La samah Allah,* God forbid something happened..."

"I know, Khaled. Cool it, *habibi.* Gigi knows the drill; she calls you if my phone is off. If that's off, she calls the landline," I tell him and pause to think. "We still have a landline, right? We didn't cancel it, right?"

His laugh fills the apartment. "Yes, we still have a landline," he confirms. "I pay the bill. Although, to tell you the truth, I haven't heard it ring in a while."

I rush to the furthermost corner of the living room, where on the floor rests our home phone. I pick it up and put it to my ear. "All good," I say in relief after hearing the dial tone.

"So, we're really doing this?!" asks Khaled, still in awe, as if such a suggestion is unworldly.

To show good faith, I power off my mobile phone first, give it to him, and point to the black screen. "See? It's off. Take it and hide it with yours. I don't want to see either all day. No phones, no internet, total blackout. Deal?"

"Deal, I guess," he says in resignation. I see him power his phone off, go inside for a few seconds, and come back, holding his hands out in a childish gesture for me to see they are empty.

I smile at him warmly. "Khaled, we need this. We really do."

"I know," he replies without hesitation. "We do."

"Now, why don't you come here? I want to hug you," I demand.

He walks into my outstretched arms and hugs me back. A minute or so later, while still in his arms, I ask, "What are you going to feed me?"

2

Today is Friday, Areej's day, but Areej is on a long weekend trip with a friend to attend the wedding of another friend's daughter in the Movenpick Hotel in the Dead Sea. She had called Khaled a week earlier to inquire if Khaled could manage without her this weekend as she, regretfully, would not be in Amman. And is it ok if her baby spends the weekend without her? And that she will make him her famous *Maqlouba* when she sees him soon. Khaled assured her that she must go and have fun, and he will see her Friday next.

I woke earlier this morning to the sound of his key in the lock. I jumped out of bed with the full intent of accosting him in the hallway. With a quick glance at my nightstand and after blowing kisses to three objects resting on it, I rushed to him and laid out my proposal.

Now, we sit on the couch with my head in his lap. "How are you?" I ask.

"I'm good," he replies.

---

* Maqlouba (literally translates to upside-down): A traditional Middle Eastern dish consisting of meat, rice and vegetables such as cauliflower, potatoes, tomatoes, and eggplant cooked together in a pot. It is served when the pot is turned "upside-down."

"Lovely generic answer. Thank you for that," I say, laughing. "Now, can you please answer me straight?"

"What do you want me to say? I really am fine," he laughs too.

"Ok, that's great, *habibi*," I say and fall silent. We remain like that, with my head in his lap, his fingers playing with my hair, saying nothing for a few minutes.

"How about you? How are you?" he breaks the silence.

"Oh, I'm great. Rainbows and chocolate fountains everywhere. Happy happy happy," I answer joylessly.

He gives me a mirthless chuckle. "I'm sorry, Nuha," he says. "I'm sorry for keeping you at arm's length. I just feel you have enough on your plate without me burdening you with more of my unsolvable problems."

"I'm offended, Khaled!" I tell him. I feel his thighs stiffen under my head and I sit up to face him. "Let me stop you before you try to find excuses for what you just said," I continue. "I'm not here to solve your problems. I'd have solved mine if I knew how to solve problems." Simultaneous chuckles erupt, which help to soften the mood. "But you know you can tell me anything, and you know that I listen, and just getting stuff off your chest is enough in my experience, knowing that someone understands you. At least that's how it's been for me, Khaled, for God knows how many years now."

"It's how we help each other—we talk, and we listen. I know that, Nuha. We help each other by just being there," he explains.

"Exactly! So? What's stopping you?" I look at him with pleading eyes. "Please, no more hiding. Let's get it all out today."

"It's just... I don't know. You don't like him," he says, taking in my reaction. Then, observing my startled look, he continues, "Don't like is not strong enough an expression. You actually hate his guts so much that you can't be objective about anything concerning him."

I gape at him but say nothing.

"I'm sorry, Nuha, but that's the truth."

I am still silent, trying to contemplate what he just said.

"And I believe it's partly my fault," he continues. "I gave you all the ammunition to hate him, and I shouldn't have because he's not a bad person, Nuha. He's not!"

"I don't hate him," I whisper, barely audible.

"Yes, you do, *habibti*, you do, and I'm to blame, and for that, I'm sorry."

"But he upsets you," I interject, and try to find a foothold to justify why I feel the way I do.

"He doesn't!" Khaled cuts me off. "And if he has in the past, I've forgiven him. So, for me, you should too, please, Nuha."

Again, I am searching for a comeback and not finding an appropriate one when Khaled resumes, "And so, I quit talking because every time I wanted to, I knew that half of our exchange would be spent with me defending him instead of talking about the main issue, so I stopped."

"I see..."

"I used to bitch about my problems; I wanted your empathy. That was thoughtless of me, I admit. I should have given you the whole picture. He's a good man, Nuha. Please believe me."

"But when he's around, he's always in a sour mood, and your mood is even worse. He's not good for you, Khaled," I say, trying to get through to him and make him see what I see when I see them together.

"God! You are so stubborn!" Khaled's voice rises. "See?! That's exactly what I'm talking about. When it comes to him, you don't want to listen. You didn't hear a word I said. You have a picture in your obstinate head and don't want to change it." With those words, Khaled gets up and starts for the kitchen.

"Ok, I'm sorry. Come back." However, he doesn't return, so I get up and follow him to the kitchen.

I walk in. Khaled is leaning on the counter; his hands are crossed at his chest, and he looks at me.

"I'm sorry," I say again. "I want us to talk."

"I can do that. I can talk all day and night, but it's useless if you don't listen."

"I'm listening. I promise you I will listen. Just make me understand because I don't understand what has changed."

He inhales deeply and lets it out slowly. He looks over my shoulder into the distance. "Nothing has changed, Nuha. It has always been like this: I felt sorry for myself and wanted your pity, and I got more than I bargained for."

"I still don't understand."

"You love me, and you care for me, but instead of helping me get over my pettiness and see things clearly, it backfired, and you became obsessed with protecting me and fighting my battles and blind to the truth."

"Ok, Khaled, I get what you're saying," I say. "I understand your words. But can I say it how I see it, and you bear with me and hear me out till the end?"

"Go ahead, I'm all ears," he says with sincerity. It is clear that Khaled truly wants this issue resolved, and he would do anything I ask to reach this goal.

"Ok, so this is how I see it," I start, settling myself on one of the kitchen stools, feeling confident that, finally, we are getting somewhere. "He comes over, always scowling. Always finding fault in everything. Nothing pleases him, and I see you bend backward to please him and never succeed. He's always disgruntled with me mainly, even though I only had good things to say to him from the beginning. I try to please him in every way possible. I try to soothe him when he's angry, and for what? He treats me like I'm the maid around here without even a sideways glance." I fall silent, and I gauge Khaled's demeanor. Good to his word, he says nothing and waits for me to finish. "So, now you tell me, how have I misread the situation?" I look at Khaled, who is looking at me with sad eyes. I go to him and hug him. Just seeing that unhappiness makes my heart ache. "I'm sorry. I really am."

"No! Don't be sorry. I'm not. I'm glad we're talking," he replies. "Have you finished?"

"Pretty much, yes."

"*Habibti*, I'm not going to contradict anything you said. It doesn't look good for him. I agree with you, but I want you to listen to me, ok?"

"Ok-ay..." I reply hesitantly.

"He's a good man, Nuha, and a caring man too. I know this; trust me on it. Growing up, he didn't have an easy life, and his life recently got even worse. So, please give him another chance, for me." His pleading voice has an edge to it.

"What are you saying, that he will miraculously become another person? Or that I'm so blind that nothing of what I told you happened?" I ask uncertainly. "Khaled, you're asking me to unsee what is in front of me."

"I don't want you to see or unsee anything. Nothing. Whatever I say now isn't going to help. I want you to give him another chance. Can you do that?"

I say nothing and just look through the window onto the street behind Khaled's back. Seconds of stillness tick by.

"He is jealous, Nuha!" Khaled raises his voice passionately, breaking the oppressive silence. "Can't you see that?! Don't you realize he sees us together and begrudges what we have? He doesn't get us. He doesn't understand how we work together. I will talk to him, I will make him understand your point of view, but please, one more chance. That's all I'm asking." He stops talking and surveys me. "If you want me to beg, I will," he adds and laughs nervously. "I will!"

I consider this and know deep down that it won't work, but I don't tell him that. Be that as it may, I will do anything for Khaled. "Ok, of course. Whatever you say."

His smile of relief makes me happy. "How about I cook dinner for the three of us this week?" he asks rhetorically, his mind already on something else. Then, finally, he turns and walks out to the living room. "How about a movie marathon?"

The tone of finality in his rhetorical question suggests that the discussion has ended, at least from his perspective.

"Who goes first?" I chirp. Deep inside me, however, something frets and gnaws away.

3

We watch *The Shawshank Redemption* first, of course, Khaled's choice. Second, *Sex and the City*, the movie, my choice. I then suggested *Pride and Prejudice*, the 2005 movie, but it was vetoed because it was his turn for *A Walk in the Woods*, starring Robert Redford and Nick Nolte.

In our default movie position, my head on his lap, we watch *A Walk in the Woods*, laugh, and feel in awe of the scenery's beauty. It was our first time, and we both were dumbfounded by the beauty of the Appalachian Trail, a place I had never heard of before but fell in love with instantly.

The end credits roll, and he asks the question I knew was coming. He wasn't the only one with things to get off their chest today. "Tell me more about Zaid?" He poses the question calmly, his fingers playing with my hair, my head still on his lap.

"More?" I ask.

"Yes, more. I know some from Tea," he says.

"I see, so that's how you know his name, from Tea?" I ask and turn my head so we can talk face-to-face.

He is silent. He has a shadow of a smile on his lips. He doesn't answer and waits for me to speak.

And I tell him everything. I tell him about the first time I set eyes on Zaid. I tell him how it was comparable to an out-of-body experience, how I felt like a spectator witnessing two people meet for the first time, lock eyes, and shake hands. I try to explain how it seemed like they knew each other before meeting, and meeting each other completed them both. I think he gets me and understands what I am trying to convey. He listens without comment, and his expression alternates between interest and mild concern.

"What is it?" I ask.

He looks deep into my eyes when he says, "Be careful."

"You already told me that before," I say. "Tell me something else."

"He's a serious man, Nuha. I don't get the impression he's playing around."

A minute passes, and I don't reply. My head is back on his lap, my eyes no longer looking into his.

"He might want more than you want to give." Khaled breaks the silence.

"I know, and he does."

"So, you are willing to break his heart?"

"I don't want to, but I don't want to tell him now. Maybe later. Surely later. But I need him now, Khaled," I say, and I feel tears choking me for the first time in a very long time.

"It's ok, *habibti*. It'll be ok."

We fall into another silence. Finally, I say, "You're smoking again."

"I'll quit again," he tells me mechanically.

"When are we going to hike the Appalachian Trail?" I ask.

"Soon," he replies with his perfunctory response.

"I mean it, Khaled; I want to walk that trail." Something in my tenor alerts him because he focuses on me again.

Few people know me. The 'new me,' that is. Two are now dead; my father and grandmother knew me well, not fully understanding the motivation behind some of my actions but loving me enough to overlook my quirks. My mother knows me somewhat, and Tea also well enough. But Khaled knows me best; sometimes, I feel more than he should.

For the last ten years, since I stopped living and started only existing, I have only been to four places in total, and only along the streets to and from and around those four locations:

Big House, my apartment, The Place, and Areej's house. Just recently, one more was added to the shortlist, Zaid's place, making them now five in all. I have never veered off my course all these years, and on my first drive to Zaid's home, I had to stop three times on the side of the road to calm my breathing and get my jitters under control. On more than one occasion during that trek, I thought about finding the safest and closest detour to one of my familiar streets and abandoning the whole endeavor, but for some reason, I persevered.

So now, after I announce that I want to take a hike, and not just any walk, but one in the United States of America, anyone other than Khaled would have made light of it. He, on the other hand, gives a cautious laugh and looks at me intently. "Ok," he says after a while. "Ok," he says again with more conviction. "We are going to hike the Appalachian Trail."

The 'when' and the 'how' are not important to Khaled; what is important is that I am making plans for the first time in a very long time, not just for book reading or book signing or delivery, but instead planning for the future.

monday 3 october

today was a very special day. very very special.
Because today there was a solar eclipse. Miss mona
our science teacher siad that a solar eclipse is when
the moon comes between earth (our plant where
we live) and the sun. Miss mona showed us picture
of eclipses but siad that we should not look at it
in the sky because it is not good for the eyes. I
think miss mona is very smart. This is why I asked
her after the class finished, I said to miss mona can
I ask you a question please and miss mona siad yes
ofcourse faten you can ask me a question and I siad
why is it called the red sea but it is not red and
is blue?

Miss mona siad that seas appear blue because
wavelength of light and absorption of light and I
don't know ☹ I forgot what she siad and dear
diary I didn't understand what miss mona siad. But
when she asked me did you undersant faten? I
smiled (sheepishly) and siad yes!

The best thing that happened to me today is:

I learned about solar eclispse

I saw a solar eclipse on tv because if I look in the sky my eyes will hurt (so I didn't)

Suzy siad that her birthday is soon and she will invite me

Good night now but dear diary I still don't know why it's called the red sea ☹⇕↘

CHAPTER 15

1

I had the dream again. I am at the shore. I am not alone this time; the dog is with me, but he is older and looks tired. He stares at me wearily and then turns and walks away. I stand alone on the sand, and the red water laps at my bare feet. The sun is shining, but the wind is freezing. Zaid holds the dog in the distance and calls me to join them. Nona, come here, he says, and I say, you don't call me by that name. Never call me by that name.

I wake up with a start. I open my eyes to darkness.

Why is Zaid there? This annoys me to no end. I resent his intrusion on this dream.

By and by, I surface back to awareness and realize that it is my dream, after all, not his. However, my irritability does not abate with this knowledge. I get out of bed and sit on the edge. I look at my nightstand and take one of the photographs in my hand and plead with the face in the frame. Finally, I get up and pace. Khaled is still asleep; it is too early even for him. I head to the kitchen; the microwave timer declares it to be 3:14. Phone in hand, I make my way to the kitchen counter and sit.

After Friday's total blackout, Saturday was mayhem. Before I went to bed late Friday night, I turned my phone back on to find 213 WhatsApp messages, 65 of which were from Zaid. Two were from Tea to ask me why my phone was turned off. And the rest were from WhatsApp groups that Tea had added me to against my request to the contrary, full of their periodic uplifting-positive messages that I promptly deleted.

Zaid had taken Friday's silence as a betrayal, and my explanation to him later, which I now agree was somewhat feeble, did not sit well with him. So I spent all my busy Saturday, consumed between The Place and Big House, trying to appease him with messages that went seen but unreturned, and calls that went unanswered. He was mad at me for not alerting him first to my intentions, and come to think of it, understandably so. I admit I could have handled it better with Zaid, but what was done was done.

The microwave timer declares it now to be 3:30. It's early Sunday morning, and I need to see him. I was thinking of making tea and starting a racket to wake Khaled. My plans alter, however, and waking Khaled is not at all conducive to my new campaign. I slip off my stool and head to the bathroom as quietly as possible. I am ready to leave the house twenty minutes later, and the time on the microwave blinks at 3:52. Shoes in hand, I only put them on after I exit and lock the apartment door behind me.

Simply Red sings *Fairground* on my car's radio. I know the song well, and it might have been a favorite in my distant past.

> *"And I love the thought of coming home to you*
> *Even if I know we can't make it*
> *Yes, I love the thought of giving hope to you*
> *Just a little ray of light shining through"*

Fate has a hand in the songs the radios play. I listen and marvel at the aptness of the lyrics.

2

Zaid's place is a studio apartment above the furniture gallery he manages and owns in partnership with his mother and two older sisters. The eldest of the sisters, Shiraz, is married and lives with her husband and four children in Irbid in the north of Jordan. The younger sister, Shahinaz, still lives with their mother in the family home two blocks from the gallery.

It's about a ten-minute drive from my home to his using the fastest route, mainly because there is virtually no traffic at this time of the morning. Nonetheless, my idiosyncrasies necessitate using a different route, adding another five minutes or so to the excursion. So, at about a quarter past four in the morning, I park my car on the street in front of the closed gallery entrance.

Zaid has no knowledge of this visit and is almost undoubtedly asleep. I enter the building from the side door and run the two flights of stairs up to my destination. I knock softly at first and slightly harder the second time. Finally, with no imminent response, I bang loudly on the door. I am not afraid of rousing any neighbors because there are none. I hear footsteps from the other side of the door, and then the light above the door switches on, illuminating the stairwell. I notice the peephole in the middle of the door dim for a split second, and then I hear the door unlock.

3

Our eyes meet, and we say nothing for a while; mine are in earnest, his are still sleepy but nonetheless bewildered. I tread over the threshold without invitation, and he raises no objections but steps back to facilitate my entry. It dawns on me that I don't know what to say to him. In fact, my primary motive for visiting him was not to talk. I want to relate that I care and am sorry for upsetting him last Friday; I don't have the words, but I have other plans. However, I hesitate when I see the expression on his face. He's upset, and he's not trying to hide it. I rack my brain for something to say to ease the situation, putting on hold my original plan of leaping at him at the door and making him forget why he was ever mad at me in the first place. It's not that Zaid wasn't intensely physical.

Rather, I have come to acknowledge that physical intimacy is not enough when it involves me. He wants everything with me: not just the physical and emotional connection, but also possibly the mental.

"Hi," I say. I try to inject cheerfulness into my voice. "I've missed you."

He says nothing, but I feel him soften a little. However, not wanting to relinquish his anger all too hastily, I watch as he turns his back to me and marches to the open kitchen area, saying, "We might as well have coffee at this godawful hour."

"No," I say.

"I have tea if you want?"

"I'll have 'you' if you have it?"

His reply is swift and solemn. "You cannot do that to me again. I was worried sick. Did you know that?"

"I know now," I say.

"What worries me is that you didn't know then," he says forlornly. "I imagined the worst happened. I was frantic! How could you not have known, Nuha?"

It's all so sudden, I think. Everything is moving too fast, I think. We've only known each other for a short time, and I still suffer from the blow caused by your emotional attack on my senses. I think all this, but I tell Zaid none of it. Instead, I tentatively go to him, place my head on his chest, and say, "I will handle it differently next time, I promise."

Over the years, I've become more resolute in not compromising for anything or anyone. For this reason, I intentionally used the words 'next time' in my reply to Zaid. If he registers my meaning or not, it's not clear, but I feel his whole demeanor softening, and I sink deeper into his embrace.

"I'm wearing something you'd like," I tell him brazenly.

He loosens his grip, parts my heavy wool coat, and looks at my plain sweatshirt with 'The Place' printed on the front and my faded jeans. "I do like," he says.

"Well, thank you very much, baby. But I meant what's

under these," I tell him with a lascivious wink.

He grins, and I know I'm forgiven when he leisurely slips my coat off my shoulders and lets it fall to the floor, and then his hand cups my breast and squeezes it with exquisite abandon. The material of my sweatshirt and bra separate his palm from my flesh. He traces the contour of my nipple under the fabric with one thumb and languidly pinches the now hard knot with his thumb and forefinger. I press into his hand, wanting more of his touch, and move my lips toward his, needing to taste them. He moves his head back slightly; I move closer to him and feel his other hand on the nape of my neck and through my hair, steadying me, holding me back from his lips and denying me their touch. He wants me to feel his breath on my lips, but not the touch. His eyes don't leave mine. His hand slips under the sweatshirt and rests on my swollen breast. He kneads the peak through the satin material of my bra. Our skins burn for each other, but technically they are not touching. My lips mouth the word "Please..." and he understands but won't relent easily. With a quick flick of his wrist, his hand is now inside my bra, skin on bare skin. I feel the warmth of his palm, and his squeeze becomes harder and rougher.

The pad of his thumb is teasing my hard nipple, drawing circles around it and chafing the tip. Again, I move closer to his lips, and he resists. I try again, and he holds my head steady. I can feel his breath, but still cannot touch his lips. I need more, and the palm of his hand on my flesh is no longer enough. My other breast is screaming for attention; my whole body is begging for it. Finally, his hand on my neck relents, and my head jerks forward to take his lips with mine. I'm hungry for him; his tongue slips inside my mouth, and I suck it. My body attacks his, and I rub myself along the length of his build with a complete lack of inhibition. I can feel his hardness pressing into me, and I double the friction. The clothes that separate us only manage to fuel the fantasy of the pleasure to follow.

I'm in a frenzy now; I want everything all at once. He retakes control and steadies me, whispering, "Easy, baby..." and lets his hand slide down my jeans. He feels my dampness and need, and this time doesn't make me wait. He withdraws his hand, swiftly slides his arm under my knees, and carries me to the bed.

4

When *Abu Zaid* died three years earlier, his legal heirs, wife, and three children decided to keep the family business and, by consensus, appointed Zaid to manage the gallery. After subtracting all other expenses and Zaid's salary, subsequent profits from the company were to be dispensed according to *Sharia**.

For the first year after his father's death, Zaid lived in his childhood home with his mother and sister, Shahinaz. But soon after, notwithstanding his mother's displeasure, Zaid moved to his own place. Despite the family's close-knit and conservative upbringing, *Um Zaid* relented after a short while as she considered it a win-win situation; his new place was close enough for her to keep an eye on him but distant enough for him to feel independent.

Zaid wants to tell me everything about himself and his life. He has already told me about his mother, sisters, friends, and growing up on several occasions. He talked a lot about his father, how he created the business, and how it flourished. He explained why he studied business administration so that one day he could run the business with his father. But, unfortunately, fate had it that the responsibility of management dropped on him sooner than he had desired or imagined.

He talks with such passion and keenness that I cannot

---

* Sharia: The Islamic religious law derived from the religious precepts of Islam, particularly the Quran and the Hadith (records of the words and actions of prophet Mohammad).

help but listen in admiration. For all the obvious reasons that I need not explain to him, nor has he ever asked me to, we never go outside in public. Our talks are almost always in his studio, either while he's cooking or we're eating or as part of our pillow talk. I listen to him intently and with interest, and as long as I don't have to reciprocate with similar anecdotes about me, then I'm fine. Whenever I feel a lull in the narrative and a pause, expecting a commentary, I murmur, nod, or ask a question to fuel his momentum. When I do share, however, it's usually about my day, stories about Tea, Saja, and The Place, but nothing about the real me, the past me, not yet.

This early Sunday morning, the sun's rays start to make their way through the window blinds. While my head rests on his chest, I hear him talk about a local artist from whom he plans to acquire paintings for the gallery. He surprises me with a request: "Tell me something about you. It seems that I'm the one always talking about my stuff."

'Way to state the obvious!' I think, but don't say. I puzzle over a response, and one jumps to mind out of the blue. It's not a declaration or an anecdote of any substance, just a question.

"Why is it called the Red Sea?" I ask.

5

As is often the case, Zaid is upset when I get up to leave. Every time, he acts like it's a surprise that I must go and that we don't have all day to frolic in total abandon. It was kind of endearing the first few times; now it's starting to border on irksome.

"Work, Zaid. I have to go to work," I tell him, slipping into my jeans.

"But it's too early. Don't go," he replies.

I try to change the subject by asking, "So, you liked my

surprise?" I regret my words as soon as they leave my lips. What am I thinking asking him about my lacy underwear?! I laugh at the expression on his face, a mixture of lust and bewilderment.

"Tantalizing," he answers me. "Come back here, and I'll show you how much."

I walk into the main room and look for my bag and coat. He follows me out of the bedroom with a towel wrapped around his midriff and nothing else. Coat on and purse in hand, I head to him and kiss him deeply.

"Any last-minute words of wisdom before I head out?" I ask humorously.

"If I tell you that leaving now will be very detrimental to your health, would you stay?" he answers seriously.

"No," I say simply.

"Ok, sexy... one more kiss then." He follows me to the door; his arms wrap around my waist, and his lips kiss my neck when I open it.

The thirty-something woman—who has Zaid's eyes and nose but not his mouth—standing in the stairwell when the door opens is clearly not pleased by what she sees.

"What's this?" she asks, trying to sound simultaneously unimpressed and appalled.

I look at the scene transpiring in front of me: Zaid clad in nothing but a towel and a small one at that, and I presume the other protagonist to be Shahinaz, Zaid's sister whom he had previously proclaimed to be three years his senior. Also, from previous talks about his family, I had gathered that Shahinaz was a branch manager for a local bank. Today she was immaculately dressed in a dark business suit over a pristine white shirt with a ruffled collar. She had on a white hijab neatly pinned around her oval face. An awkward silence ensues, and I perceive a secret exchange between the two siblings, the contents of which I am not privy to—but I can attest to it taking place just by observing body language and facial expression.

The situation was so tense that it was starting to border on laughable.

"Hello. Nice to meet you." What a stupid thing to say, yet I had to say something to break the palpable tension.

The look of contempt that I get and the derogatory words—"whore" and "bitch"—that follow, I know, aim to insult me. Yet, I could have saved her the trouble and the fight with her brother that would arise as a consequence just by telling her not to bother because I am un-insultable.

"*Sharmuta*," she says in a way a judge would pronounce a court ruling.

"Shut up!" Zaid's voice comes from behind me in a tone that I have never heard from him. I look at him, and the rage on his face worries me.

She does not answer him, but looks at me. The incredulity that she portrays is comic, but I don't dare laugh. Instead, I sidestep her and start my way down the stairs with a quick wave to Zaid and a hasty, "Bye, see you later."

"*Weskha*," she shouts after me, and I genuinely pity her for it because, unbeknownst to her, she might have just put a sizable dent in her relationship with her brother. For a reason still not fully clear to me, Zaid worships the ground I walk on, and Shahinaz will face his wrath. I actually shudder to think about it.

6

Zaid is puzzled by my total disregard for what transpired at his doorstep earlier this morning. When he visits The Place, all apologies and regret, he finds me all smiles at seeing him. Yet, he is profoundly sorry and swears that nothing like that will ever happen again. I mean the world to him, and he won't ever allow anyone in his family to forget that. He won't let me down if I only give him another chance. However, he says all this before he registers my demeanor, and at first, he doesn't understand and thinks it's too late, that he's already lost me. I think he believes that my cheerfulness is just a pretense to not lose face in front of him.

I can use one of two ways to deal with this incident; my first option is to tell Zaid not to worry because I don't care what people think and I have very thick skin, and words meant to injure or insult me are essentially useless and usually bounce right off. However, this may require me to divulge where I got the thick skin from, details I still need to be ready to share. Or, I can make Zaid grasp the situation from another angle, the side he doesn't see and is adamant about not accepting.

Tea has not made an appearance yet, and I can feel the daggers shooting out of Saja pierce my back as I move Zaid to the back room, where we can talk in private.

"When I opened your front door today, what do you think Shahinaz saw?" I ask him.

"What?! What are you talking about? She had no right..." he starts to argue.

"Listen to me, will you? What do you think she saw? Describe it to me." I repeat this time with both my hands on his shoulders, trying to calm him and communicate that this is a discussion, not a fight.

He gapes back at me mutely.

"I'll tell you, Zaid. Please listen to me. Try to see it through her eyes," I start.

"Why are you defending her?!" He's livid. "No one talks to you like that. No one!"

I can't stop myself from hugging him. A wave of intense emotion that I lack the words to define washes over me. We stand holding each other in silence. I feel a kind of protection and well-being in his arms that I'd never experienced before. But I still need to tell him what he needs to know and what he must accept.

I begin again as if there were no interruption. I speak

slowly and deliberately. "Honey, people don't see us like we see us. Do you understand me?"

When he says nothing back, I go on. "This morning, very early in the morning, I must add, your sister saw a middle-aged woman getting her neck smooched by a very hairy, scantily clad, much younger man. That young man is her only brother. It was a shock, Zaid."

He looks at me despondently.

"The hairy thing was a joke, by the way," I laugh and try to lighten the mood, but to no avail. He doesn't even crack a smile.

"You are still trying to find excuses for her," he observes. "Why?!"

"I'm stating the facts, honey. I'm trying to be realistic. She saw her brother with an older woman who had obviously spent the night, or part of it, in his home," I explain to him. "Factor in the little detail that I'm married and..." Zaid instantly averts his eyes from me when I say that last part. I continue regardless. "Ok, let me ask you something. Do you know the number one item on your mother and sister's to-do list?"

He looks at me, perplexed. "What are you talking about?"

"To find you the perfect girl. To get you married, big guy! And I'd bet my right arm that they already have a candidate, or maybe two." I see him avoid eye contact for a split second. I know that I hit the spot. "See?! I'm right, right?" I laugh.

The look of dejection on his features makes me want to hug him and make it better, but I cannot stop now. "The picture of you and me, Zaid, it's not ok. It's not a pretty picture. I'm sorry, but that's the truth. And I'm not just saying your mother and sisters might think this way. I'm saying, everyone."

"What are you saying, Nuha? Please don't..." He's angry. I can feel waves of hostility emanating from his skin. "I don't care what anyone says or sees, or whatever..."

"I just want you to know what people see when they see us together. That is all I'm saying. What we want to do about it is our decision. Yours and mine. Do you understand me now?" I say carefully.

"Nuha…" he says my name and then stops. I can see him searching for the words. I give him the time he needs, and he closes his eyes. I step closer to him; I want him to feel my proximity. "I'm not blind, Nuha. But I also don't want to see." He pulls me closer to him so that our bodies are touching. "Nuha, you are my love. My sunshine. My shelter. My home." He opens his eyes and looks into mine. "You are my all."

It must be the look in my eyes that convinces him that his message got through. He leans into me and kisses me eagerly and with urgency. His lips and teeth find my right earlobe. He bites me there and whispers, "Come home with me now."

"Work…" My voice breaks. I try again. "We have work, both of us."

"This evening?" he whispers, his mouth too close to my ear.

"Your tongue… do that again…" I murmur.

He obliges me. And I hear him take a deep breath, trying to regain control. "Promise me this evening."

"I promise," I say and mean it.

He moves to the door, but before he leaves, I say, "Honey, by the way, I like hairy, so no heroic measures, ok?"

Only then do I hear the throaty laugh that I'm starting to crave daily.

thursday 13 october

Tomorrow is suzy's birthday! I'm very very happy and excited! (☺) Suzy siad that because I am her best friend she invited me the first from all the class. She invited everyone after she invited me. I siad to her why invit the boys? Boys are stupid. And she siad to me that her mother siad that she should invite evryone.

My mommy is taking me today to buy suzy a birthday present. I still don't know what I want to give her. Mommy siad if it was your birthday what would you want suzy to get you?

I siad a dog! Mommy siad that suzy's parents might not like that because dogs are a big responsipility.

Then I siad a doll house! And daddy siad remember that I am not made of money. Silly daddy! Ha ha ha of course he's not made of money!! He is made of bone and blood and skin like everyone else. And then mommy and daddy laugh and then mommy siad how about you give suzy a board game?

Best thing that happened to me today:

1. Tommorow is suzy's birthday yayayayaya

2. I'm going to give suzy a board game called Guess who? I am sure she will love it I'm very excited

3. Daddy bought a game for us to play at home. It is called UNO

4. I won 2 times in UNO. Mommy won 1 time in UNO. Daddy like me 2 times. And M zero! Hahahah

Good night dear diary

CHAPTER 16

1

I decide to sleep in Big House Monday evening. Khaled will join me there Tuesday for lunch, as is the custom. My mother called me this morning, and we talked. She said she missed me, and I told her, "I miss you too, Mama. I passed by Big House yesterday afternoon, *habibti*. You should be sick of me by now."

"I miss you all the time, Nuha," she replied simply.

I felt my heart tighten at that statement and hence my decision.

Gigi greets me at the door. First, she informs me that Mama went to lie down because she felt lightheaded, then tells me, "She's always tired," pauses for a few seconds, then continues, "There is something else you should call Doc Jareer about, ma'am."

"What is it, Gigi?" I try to keep the alarm out of my voice.

"I noticed that her legs and ankles are bigger. Like they are balloons," she explains, then adds with unmistakable distress, "This morning, her slippers wouldn't fit her feet!"

"Yes, I will call Doctor Jareer." I agree with her, remove my mobile phone from my bag, and sit at the kitchen table.

"And don't forget to tell him she's always tired and weak."

"You can tell him all you want when he's here, Gigi. I'll ask him to pass by."

About an hour and a half later, while my mother is still napping, Doctor Jareer enters my mother's bedroom carrying his doctoring bag that never fails to amaze me by the deluge of medical paraphernalia it contains. She stirs when she hears the commotion, and the first thing I notice is her eyes searching for me. When she spots me, a smile of relief crosses her features, and I cannot help but be grateful that I decided to be here for her today and as long as she needs me.

Doctor Jareer examines, prods, and pokes my mother and asks her, as well as Gigi, the unofficial head nurse, a million questions. Later, over coffee in the living room, while my mother rests inside, and in the company of my Young Aunts who insist on taking coffee with *ahsan duktor belkawn* the best doctor in the universe, he explains what ails my mother.

According to Doctor Jareer, my mother's new symptoms are a consequence of her previous medical problems, and her heart is no longer capable of pumping blood to the body as well as it should, and because it's not doing its work correctly, fluid is backing up in her legs and feet, causing them to swell. I'm concentrating on his words, but in my peripheral vision, I notice that the Young Aunts simultaneously inspect their feet, and Fatima lifts one up as far as it goes to examine it more closely.

"So, what do we do, Doc? What do you suggest?" I ask.

"You're doing everything that can be done, Nuha," he replies. "Your mother also is a model patient, even if a little stubborn." Then when Gigi comes in with a tray of coffee cups, he adds, "Gigi is a godsend to your mother; I wish I had an assistant like her in my practice." His praises of Gigi are genuine and sincere. In turn, Gigi beams, having clearly heard his approval of her. He then pauses and looks at my aunts, seemingly not wanting to leave them out. He adds, "Feryal and Fatima are a great comfort to Sarah, always at her bedside entertaining her, and that's just what she needs." The Aunts look at each other and nod in agreement. Gigi, on the other hand, looks at me and rolls her eyes.

Doctor Jareer addresses me as he stands to leave, "Nuha, I will write a prescription for a new drug that will help. I also discussed with Gigi a few adjustments to your mother's current medications. I can go over them with you if you like."

"There's no need if you told Gigi. She'll fill me in later.

Thank you so much, Doctor Jareer."

He pats my arm and adds, "I'll call in a few days. If things haven't improved by then, we'll discuss further testing, but I don't see the need for that now."

"And I'll call you if *la samah Allah* God forbid things get worse," I tell him as I walk him to the door.

Just at the door, he turns and looks at me hesitantly. "Nuha, my dear, I just want to say that your mother *Allah ytawel be'omurha* may God prolong her life. She is..."

I cut him off and say, "I know, Doc. I know. My mother is old and frail and sick, and we should expect anything. You have done a lot for us over the years, for all the family, for me even..." My words falter. "Anyway, what I want to say is that your medical opinion to me is the best there is. You needn't say more. God bless you."

2

I don't have an overnight bag, but it's not my first impromptu stay at Big House without one, so I must have a change of clothes or maybe two tucked away somewhere. In the evening, I call Khaled and ask him to bring a few more with him tomorrow, as I expect to spend more than just one night here. He is concerned and asks me if I want him to come over immediately instead of waiting until tomorrow to see us.

"No need, *habibi*, you don't need to leave work. I know you're working late tonight. I'll see you tomorrow at lunch."

"You're sure Sarah is doing well, Nuha?" he asks.

"Yes, I'm sure. She's watching something on TV right now, the one in the living room. Well, actually, the TV is on, but what actually is happening is that the three of them are bickering about something or another. I can't keep up." I laugh.

Khaled chuckles and says, "See you later then, babe. Take care."

"Khaled!" I know he will be able to sense the tension in my voice. "One more thing. Since I'll be staying more than one night, can you..."

He doesn't let me finish. "Of course, Nuha. Of course. I'll bring them with your clothes."

"Thank you," I say with genuine gratitude.

"Of course, *habibti*," he repeats.

3

Tea, dressed in a woolen pink formfitting dress with ruffles around the neckline and the cuffs, comes over in the evening to visit my sick mother. However, my mother had retired to her room earlier, so Tea sits with the Young Aunts in the living room, and I pretend to make the coffee. I instead chat with Zaid on the phone while Gigi makes the coffee.

"*Omri!*" he exclaims once he hears my voice.

"How are you?" I ask him.

"Worried about you. Can't stop thinking of you. Missing you like crazy," comes his reply.

"What are you doing?" I ask.

"Finishing the accounts. I'll close up soon," he replies. "Do you want me to come over?"

"Oh, Zaid, I wish I could inhabit the same universe you live in," I say flippantly. "How do I introduce you to my aunts? What do I tell my mother?" I humor him.

"Nuha, I don't want to see your aunts," he says in a severe tone, startling me and causing me to hesitate. I instantly regret my thoughtlessness.

I remain silent, which prompts him to go on. "I'm not an irrational teenager. I don't understand why you might think that I am. Do you think I don't know it would be unseemly for me to barge inside your mother's house?" he chides. "I miss you. I just want to pass by and see you at the door, if just for a minute. Make sure you are fine. That's all I ask. Or asked, past tense, because clearly, that's not going to happen now."

I'm lost for words. "Honey, I was joking…"

Zaid doesn't let me finish, "Nuha, no, you weren't joking. You act as if I'm delusional. I know this is not the time to be arguing about this. But this pretense that you are all rationality and I'm an illogical fool regarding what's happening between us is irritating."

I hear rustling behind me and turn to find Gigi with the coffee tray in hand, looking at me. I gesture for her to take the coffee and serve it in the living room. Then, pointing to the phone in my hand, I mouth the words "important call." She turns and walks away, and I cross the hallway, where I find a chair and sit down. I can hear Zaid's breathing on the line but ask anyway, "Are you still there?"

"I'm here," he replies. I hear a hint of despair in his voice, which saddens me. I want to say something to make it better between us. Never was my intention to upset him the way I did. But before I say anything, he asks, "How's your mother now?"

"Stable. She's sleeping."

"I'm glad. I hope she gets better soon." Zaid takes a long, audible breath and says, "Sorry for talking the way I did."

"It's ok, honey. I'm sorry for upsetting you the way I did."

"Are you busy?"

"We have time to talk, if that's what you're asking," I reply, hoping that we can resolve whatever is troubling him right now.

"I know exactly what we are, Nuha," he starts. His voice is mellow and assured. "I know exactly how it looks. I know you are married, even if I don't always talk about it. It isn't my favorite topic."

I listen, and I am struck by the assurance of his words. I was wrong; I admit this now.

"I know his name is Khaled," he continues. "I also know

he is the luckiest man in the world because you are his. And it is an insult that you think that if I don't talk about it, that means I don't acknowledge it. Nuha, I understand our situation is impossible. I know the danger you could be in, and I hate myself for it, but I can't help it. The other day, I told you I'm not blind, but I choose not to see because being with you feels right and completes me."

He waits for me to say something, but I don't. What can I say to him? How am I ever going to make him understand?

"I know your husband isn't with you at your mother's tonight because you already told me in an earlier phone call, as you recall. And that's why I suggested I pass by to see you. Because I miss you, and because every minute I don't see you, I feel it's a minute wasted. I don't know how else to explain to you that I love you!"

"Come over," I say. "I'll be waiting, baby. I miss you too." And then a few seconds later, when he doesn't reply, but I know that he's still on the line, I plead, "Please!"

4

Sometime later, I sit on a chair under the portico. I hear the faint laughter of Tea and the Young Aunts coming from behind the closed front door of the house. I wish silently that they won't disturb my mother. Still, I'm confident if there is any possibility of that, Gigi would have already alerted me and put a stop to it.

It's chilly, and I wrap myself in one of my mother's shawls; the familiar smell of *alsabun alnabulsi* fills my nostrils. Nostalgia envelopes me, as this was also the smell of my grandmother. I listen to approaching cars in the hope that one of them is Zaid's, and the hope ebbs away as, one by one, they pass me and continue on their way. I sit like that for about half an hour. Finally, when I'm about to get up and go check on my mother, I glance through a gap in the trees to see a black Mercedes park in the distance, and the familiar large figure of Zaid emerging from it. I get up from my chair but don't go to him; I watch him as he walks to me, enters the main gate, and walks up the few steps to where I stand.

His face is a mask; I cannot read him. It's dark by now, and only the soft portico light is on. He walks closer, and his two hands enclose mine. I let him with no hesitation. His hands are warm and rough, and I feel a twinge of longing to walk closer and let him enfold me whole and not just my hands, but instead, I stand my ground.

"*Omri*, your hands are so cold," he says hoarsely.

"I've been sitting outside for a while," I explain.

"I wasn't sure I wanted to come," he confesses, not meeting my eyes but looking instead at my hands in his.

"I'm glad you did," I interject without hesitation.

He rubs his thumb along my jawline, and I lean my face into his touch. His eyes meet mine now, and I can see the warmth and love in them even in the dim light.

He takes a long, leisurely look at his surroundings. "So, this is the house you grew up in," he says.

Although the statement was not meant as a question, I answer him, "No, not exactly. I spent much of my childhood here, but it wasn't my childhood home. This is my grandfather's house, my father's father. We call it Big House."

I look at Zaid as he tries to digest what I just said. "But now your mother lives here, right?" he asks.

I can see why things may confuse anyone not intricately involved in our family drama. So, I explain, "When my grandfather passed away, my grandmother lived here with her youngest two, the twins, known to all as the Young Aunts. You met them, by the way, at The Place."

"Yes, I remember them. So, those were your *young* aunts?" he asks with a slight brow raise.

"Well, certainly! They are only seventy-three, and many

good years hopefully to look forward to, being that their mother lived to be a hundred and five, and they are adamant about following in her footsteps," I say, suppressing a grin.

"Good for them. *Allah yaetihum tul alumr* may God grant them longevity," he says.

"Which brings me back to my mother." I continue the narrative, observing Zaid's interest in the subject and using it as a pretense to avoid more touchy topics. "When my grandmother got older and weaker, my father decided to move back to Big House, my mother didn't mind the move, and now, a decade after that move, the house's occupants are my twin aunts, my mother, and Gigi." I omit from my story that I was the primary deciding factor for our final move to Big House. But, I promise myself here and now that one day soon he will know—I must tell him about my 'bad period.' He has earned the right to finally know me, the real me, and then he can decide if he still wants to love me.

"Gigi?" he asks.

"Another story for another day," I laugh.

We chat a little more, Zaid and me. True to his word, the exchange does not go beyond the perfunctory questions about my day and my mother's health. With one last lingering squeeze of my hand, Zaid bids me a good night and promises to call me early the following day.

I walk him down the few steps to the front entrance. The tall spruce trees shield us from any pedestrians who may be strolling by. So, when I come eye to eye with Khaled at the gate just as Zaid is about to open it, it's quite a shock.

A few seconds follow our initial eye contact. Khaled then holds out a large backpack to me and says in a very calm, nonchalant tone, "I know I said I'll bring them tomorrow, but I thought you'd prefer if you had them tonight." I take the bag from his hand, and a second later, he asks, "Is Sarah asleep or awake?"

"Asleep," I hurriedly say, then recollect myself. "Or at least most probably is."

"I'll see her tomorrow then; I must be off," he says, returning to his car. Then he stops and turns to look at me, and says, this time with a different tone of voice, a mixture of incredulity and clean-up-this-mess reprimand, "Areej called, and when I told her about Sarah, she said she would pass by Big House on her way home from the clinic."

Not through any of this exchange does Khaled look at Zaid or acknowledge him in any way.

"I'm sorry. I'm sorry," I say to a horror-stricken Zaid after Khaled disappears from view.

It's as if Zaid doesn't hear me. He retakes my hands in his and squeezes them. His face is a mixture of alarm and concern. "Are you ok? Will you be alright? What can I do?"

I see the anguish in his features. How will I make him understand?

"I'm ok. I'll be ok. Don't worry about me," I respond.

"How can I not worry?!" he asks. His voice is full of despair.

"Zaid, look at me. Can you do that? Look at me..." Finally, he stops fidgeting and looks at me. "Sweetie, I promise you, I'll be fine. But you must leave now. We'll talk soon. Real soon. There is a lot you need to know, but not now. Good night." I say this while looking at him, then turn my back and run up the steps.

5

Gigi is helping my mother up when I enter the bedroom. I place the backpack on the bed and go over to my mother's side to see if I can assist. With the free hand that isn't in Gigi's grasp, my mother shoos me away, insisting that she doesn't need help at all, and Gigi would be doing everyone a favor if only she would leave her alone and go find something useful to do. Gigi, however, does not let go of her hand, and I allow them to pass me on their way to the bathroom.

I go to my father's side of the bed, where I'll sleep for as long as I'm needed here. I unzip the bag that Khaled got for me. On top of the clothes, I find the four items that motivated him to bring the bag sooner than we agreed. He knows me. Khaled knows me so well.

I pick up my phone and dial Khaled's number. He picks up on the first ring. "What if Areej had beaten me to Big House and saw him there? What would you have done?"

His attack surprises me. "Come on, Khaled, it was not that big a deal," I plead with him. "It could have been anyone. A delivery guy or someone."

"*Ya Allah*! If this is how you look at a delivery person while he holds your hands, we are really in trouble!" He is almost shouting now.

I say nothing for a while, and he does the same. A minute or maybe more passes, and then I say, "Thank you for the stuff. I appreciate it. I really do."

"I knew you would," he answers me, his voice calmer.

Returning to the main topic. "I'll be more careful in the future. I admit that was careless of me," I say.

"I love you, Nuha. I don't want anything to jeopardize what we have." I hear the sincerity in his voice now.

"I promise you it won't happen again," I assure him.

"How's Sarah?" he asks.

"She just got up from her nap, and I can hear her arguing with Gigi, but I'm not sure about what exactly." I'm laughing now.

"I'll see you tomorrow, *habibti*," he says.

"See you. That's the doorbell. It must be Areej. Take care, *habibi*." I end the call and run to the door to welcome my mother-in-law.

Later that night, while my mother sleeps and I prepare for bed, I place the items that Khaled brought earlier in the evening next to me on the nightstand. Two other frames now stand next to my photo and that of my half-sister. Next to those are two notebooks, one on top of the other. The one on top has a dandelion on the cover.

187

Friday 14 october

BIRTHDAY PARTY!!!!

I had the best time at suzy's party. We had cake and we played games and suzy opened the presents and suzy liked my present the best and then suzy's mother gave us all a bag. The girls pink and the boys blue and the bags had sweets and a toy. The boys got a toy car and the girls got a small mirror and a comb set.

And then daddy came and took me home in the car and I told him: daddy, my next birthday party I want to have games and invite my friends not just gand mom and grand dad, ok? And daddy siad it is ok but I have to tell mommy because mommy is the birthday party arranger and he daddy doesn't know how to arrange anything

Silly daddy! (but I love him ☺)

I siad to mommy that in our next class with miss linda, she wants everyone to tell the class what they want to be when they grow up and why they want to be it.

And I asked mommy that I have been thinking and thinking what I want to be and I have 3 things and I don't know which one to choose?

Mommy siad what are the three things that you want to be when you grow up.

1. story writer because I like to write and I am very good at it ☺

2. a pet shop owner because I love pets (dogs, cats, fishs, rabbits, birds)

3. archaeologist (mommy told me the word when I told her I want to discover places like Petra)

Which one should I say in miss linda's class? Mommy said which one do you like the best? And daddy siad you can be an archeologist that owns a pet store and writes in her free time. And then mommy and daddy laughed and laughed.

But I still don't know what to say I want to be when I grow up. What do you think dear diary?

Best thing that happened to me today: BIRTHDAY PARTY!

Good night ☺

I cant sleep: are snakes pets? I will not sill them in my shop!

CHAPTER 17

1

Mama wakes up quite cheerful this morning, and she is the one to nudge me awake. "Wake up, sleepyhead."

I open my eyes and notice the bright sun in the room. It's already late morning, past my usual wake-up time. I look at my mother sitting up on her side of the bed. Gigi is not in the room, and her bed is made. "What time is it?" I ask, and pull myself up into a sitting position.

"After nine," Mama says with a smile. She looks happy that I slept well. "I woke up two times tonight, and you were sound asleep. You never stirred, even when Gigi made a racket," Mama says and shakes her head in the general direction of the kitchen, where Gigi supposedly is.

I remember it was a few minutes to midnight when I walked Tea and Areej to the front door, which is surprising, considering that they were there to visit a sick woman who obviously needed rest. And if it wasn't for the apparent fatigue on my mother's features, I bet they would have stayed longer. But the combination of the Young Aunts, Tea, and my mother-in-law is a force that even my sick mother couldn't resist. Their laughter was contagious, and soon after Areej arrived, even I became a spectator to the banter competition between Tea and the aunts.

This morning, Mama looks well-rested and happy. I can smell fried eggs wafting in from the kitchen, and Mama decides she wants to have breakfast there with me and not in bed. I don't tell her I'd rather not have breakfast and go to The Place, but I don't want her smile to falter, so I keep silent.

"Why don't you call Tahani and tell her you will be late today?" My mother seems to be reading my thoughts, and her voice is hopeful as she makes the request. She is one of the very few people that refer to Tea by her given name and not as Madam T, which even the Young Aunts use.

"I have a better idea," I tell her. "How about I call Tahani and tell her that I'm not coming at all today?"

The joy that appears on her face after my declaration seals the deal. I make two phone calls, one to Tea, who doesn't understand why I woke her up to tell her such nonsense. "Why do you think we have Saja? I'll tell you why. For occasions such as this, and for her winning personality," she asks and answers, laughs boisterously, ends the call without a goodbye, and most probably goes back to sleep.

The other call is to Zaid. I tell him that I miss him. I say I have to see him soon to explain what happened yesterday evening. To explain more than that. To make him understand. He hears the urgency in my voice, and I think he misconstrues it as something else, as something more ominous.

"Whatever it is, we can work it out, Nuha," he pleads. "What happened last evening..." he stops to recollect his thoughts, "was my fault. I should not have come over. It was a mistake, but I missed you so much."

"Zaid, it's ok. We just need to talk. I need to say things to you, and you need to know things about me," I say reassuringly to put his mind at ease.

"When can I see you?" he asks eagerly.

"Not sure. My mother is quite obsessed with me staying next to her. I even took today off work. But, honey, I'll call you soon. I promise."

2

Mama notices the new additions to the nightstand when she settles to rest for a while before lunch. She says nothing, but I catch her eyeing them.

"Khaled brought them last night with a bag of clothes," I tell her.

She still says nothing, so I edge over to her side and put my head on her duvet-covered lap. I feel her fingertips playing with my hair, and I let her. And then my mother says something that I never in a million years imagined she would say to me or anyone. "They say 'everything happens for a reason' but I still don't understand the reason for what happened."

Minutes of silence follow; we sit in the same position, and neither of us says a word. But then my mother says absently and in a low voice, as if she doesn't want me to hear, "And now I don't think I'm ever going to find out."

"*Allah yateke tul alomr* Mama, *habibti*, I hope you'll live to be a hundred and ten," I say calmly but loud enough for her to hear. After another minute or two of silence, I add, "Mama, there is no reason. It was all a waste. And 'everything happens for a reason' is bullshit!"

Be that as it may, the adage 'everything happens for a reason' is an inherent part of my mother's make-up, making it difficult for her to just consent quietly to my offhand remark that it is bullshit. My head is in her lap, but I can feel the mechanics of her brain working to find a comeback. "You wouldn't be here..." she tells me cautiously.

I lift my head off her lap and gaze into her eyes. "Please, no. Please don't finish that sentence."

But she gives no heed to my plea. "If your sister didn't die, then your father and I would never have married, and I wouldn't have had you."

"I wish you never had me. I wish I never was. I hate me!" I cry.

"Don't say that!" she admonishes. "I love you. You are the reason for my life. I'm sorry for everything, *habibti*." Her breath catches, and I am aware of her effort to continue. "I'm sorry for what happened to you. I wish I could take it away and take away your pain, but hard as it is for you, I'm not sorry I had you, and I'm not sorry that I love you more than my life." The determination in her eyes is enough to render me silent.

I look into her precious, weary features and hug her frail body to mine. I don't say anything more because it's a hopeless argument we have had varied versions of over the years. No agreement has ever been reached, nor is there hope for one.

"How about you rest for a bit before Khaled comes over in a few hours? The sun is out; how about lunch on the balcony if it's not too cold?" I ask my mother, trying, as usual, to tiptoe around our sensitive topics.

"I'm resting, but I don't want to nap. I want to talk to you," she says. And then, not for the first time today, my mother says something else to stun me. "About two months after your father passed away, Lubna called the house, and I picked up her call." She stops and looks at my dazed face. "Your father's first wife," she adds in clarification.

"I know who Lubna is, Mama," I say.

"She told me that she'd heard about Sameer's passing and had always known Big House's landline number by heart." My mother looks at me and smiles. "We had a long talk, but I never told you about it. It wasn't... I don't know why I didn't tell you about it. I'm sorry, Nuha." I can hear the contrition in her voice.

"Oh, *habibti*. It's ok. Don't upset yourself about it now. It's been years! Tell me about it if you want," I say, trying to soothe her.

"It's just that at the time, you were still... you know..." She falters, still trying to find an excuse for what she feels was a misstep on her part.

"I was still in the caustic phase of my life, you mean? Yes, Mama, I probably was. Maybe it was a wise decision then that you didn't tell me." I attempt to put her mind at ease. "So, what did she say? How many years has it been now?" I make a quick calculation. "Wow! Almost seven."

My mother starts to tell me the tale of the long-past phone call that had taken place between her and her husband's first wife. Throughout her narrative, I do not ask questions or interject in any way, not even during the moments she lapses to collect her thoughts or catch her breath. Instead, I let her speak. I lie beside her, her hands in her lap and one of mine on top of them.

3

After the divorce was finalized, Lubna lived in Kuwait City with her parents and brother Waleed. A few years later, Waleed got married, and after he and his wife had their first-born, he signed a work contract with a company in the United Kingdom and soon after moved there with his wife and baby. Lubna remained with her parents. She went through grief counseling initially, but after a while, she stopped going, and her parents didn't push her into it. Then, she tried to return to teaching but found out she couldn't keep it up and stopped after two school semesters. So instead, she occupied her time with extensive reading and long walks. She tried to write her experience several times, but ended up burning every attempt. They were too painful to keep.

About five years after the divorce, *Abu Waleed* was diagnosed with prostate cancer and died about six months after that. *Um Waleed* and Lubna lived together for about a year in Kuwait. By then, Waleed was well established in the UK and suggested that his mother and sister leave Kuwait and reside close to him. At first, *Um Waleed* was hesitant, but Lubna secretly wished for a change. Soon after, and because of Waleed's insistence, they both made the move.

Lubna gave teaching another go. This time offering private Arabic lessons to the children of Arab families living in the UK. She succeeded and made a name for herself doing it. She soon met and got to know a Jordanian widower who lived and worked in London. He had a boy, about eight years old, and a girl, four years old. She started giving them lessons, and almost a year later, this man asked her to marry him, and she accepted.

Lubna was forty-three when she married for the second time and, in the beginning, was happy to take care of and raise her newfound family, and although she wasn't opposed to the idea of having another child, when she found herself pregnant, she had a hard time of it in the beginning. She started having anxiety attacks and needed psychological help and a lot of support from her family. However, she soon had a healthy baby boy named Motaz.

Life went on as life does. Lubna raised her three children; the eldest boy left for university, and a few years later, the girl followed. When Motaz was eighteen, he too left for university and became a civil engineer. All three are now married with children of their own. She has seven grandchildren in all.

It was Lubna's husband who informed her of Sameer's death. He subscribed to *Al Ra'i* online newspaper and had read his obituary there. Lubna had felt profound sadness at the news, but didn't know what to do about it. Then a couple of months passed, and one afternoon she decided to ring Big House's number, which she never forgot. She didn't even know if it still worked or if anyone still lived in Big House, or if there was a Big House still standing. But she convinced herself she had nothing to lose, so she rang the number, and Sarah picked up.

4

My mother falls silent and is lost in thought. Then she says, "Now if I recall correctly, she didn't speak initially. She was silent. I had to ask, 'Who is this?' several times before she did speak."

I am still silent beside my mother with my eyes closed. I try to picture the image of my father's first wife. The image I saw a long time ago in a black-and-white photograph was that of a pretty smiling woman with dark, wavy, shoulder-length hair parted in the middle.

"I remember now exactly what she said at first. She didn't introduce herself," my mother continues, "she said, '*Ta'zii al hara lakum*' my deepest condolences. I thanked her and asked to whom I was speaking. Only after she was confident that she had the correct number did she introduce herself. I remember she simply said, 'I'm Lubna,' and then a second later, 'I hope I'm not intruding. Who am I speaking to?' So I told her who I was. She apologized again for invading our privacy, and I told her that it was a pleasure to hear from her, and I meant it."

"I bet she was relieved she didn't get one of the aunts," I say, breaking my silence, and my mother laughs weakly, coughs, and laughs again.

"Actually, *habibti*, at the end of our conversation, that was exactly what she told me!" my mother exclaims, still chuckling.

"I knew it!" I say in amusement.

"She told me that she was afraid that one of Sameer's sisters might answer, and she was anxious they wouldn't want to speak to her and that she secretly wished that I would pick up," my mother tells me, and then in a low voice adds, "or you."

When I say nothing, my mother continues, "She had heard that Sameer had had a daughter."

"Had she heard anything else about me?" I ask softly, unable to keep the melancholy out of my voice.

"Yes, *habibti*. She knew all about it." The sorrow is evident in my mother's words. "And I heard her cry."

"Lubna cried?" I ask dubiously.

"Yes, she did," Mama answers. "That's how our phone call ended. I didn't know what to do or say, Nuha. She cried for

Sameer, I guess, for her Faten, for you, for life in general. And then, the call ended. She never called again, and I didn't get her number. And that was that."

5

"Is it ok if I cook dinner at our place for the three of us tomorrow evening?" Khaled whispers to me while we sit for lunch around the kitchen table. It was too cold for the balcony, after all.

A few seconds tick by, and I have no idea what he's talking about, and then it hits me. Ah, yes! Of course, the dinner I had promised Khaled to attend to reconsider and reassess my earlier verdict about a person I had already established as unworthy. I close my eyes and will the cynicism out of my thoughts. I have promised Khaled, and I owe him that much; he has stood by me in much worse circumstances. "Sure, *habibi*. Mama has improved on the new prescription. One evening away is going to be ok."

My mother hears us and confirms my words to Khaled. "Yes, I'm so much better, and Nuha doesn't need to stay here every night."

Khaled interjects, and I can sense the guilt in his voice. "*Hayati*, it's only for one evening, I promise you. It's just that this very good friend of ours is in Amman for just a few days, and we want to have him over for dinner."

"What are you making him?" Feryal asks.

"Probably my world-famous *freekeh** stuffed chicken," Khaled answers with pride, as Khaled usually does when discussing his culinary skills.

"Are we invited?" Fatima inquires eagerly.

"No!" Khaled and I answer in unison.

---

* Freekeh: A cereal food made from green durum wheat that is roasted and rubbed to create its flavor.

6

The light is on in the bedroom, and it is still early. I read a page from the notebook with the dandelion-adorned cover. From my mother's slow and regular breathing and closed eyes, I suspect she is napping. I turn another page, and in my peripheral vision, I glimpse her eyes flutter open.

"Can't sleep? Am I making too much noise?" I ask.

"I wasn't sleeping," she answers me quickly.

"You looked so peaceful. I thought you were."

"I'm thinking. I always think about you, Nuha."

From years of experience, it is after statements like this one that my guard instinctively rises. More often than not, they are followed by another declaration that I usually don't want to hear, think about, or debate in any way or form.

My instincts don't fail me, and just as I thought, my mother tells me what she's thinking and what I do not want to hear. "It's not too late. I was forty-seven when I had you, and earlier, when we talked about Lubna, she must have been your age now or maybe a couple of years older when she had Motaz. So, it's not too late to have a baby in your forties, Nuha." My mother winds down after her speech but doesn't look my way. I can feel her exhaustion from the effort it took her and the nerve she had to assemble to approach this subject.

I know that my mother realizes this might be her last futile attempt on the topic. Still, she makes her pitch anyway, an endeavor she attempts every few years. She probably also expects my answer to be identical to my answers on earlier similar occasions: silence and complete disregard. However, I decide to tell her what she wants to hear this time.

"We're thinking about it," I say.

"Thinking about it?" she probes with a touch of excitement.

I go a step further. "Working on it."

The joy on my mother's **lovely** face was worth the complete and utter lie I just fabricated.

Monday 17 october

Miss linda asked us to say what we want to be when we grow up. 4 boys siad they wanted to be engineers and 5 boys siad they wanted to be doctors. One boy siad he wanted to make space rockets and that when he grows up he wants to go to America to make space rockets there. 2 boys siad they wanted to be inventors and miss linda asked them what do you want to invent? And they siad they don't know what yet but when they grow up they will decide what to invent because they wanted to be millionares and now it is too early to know what the market needs. Miss linda siad they were very ambicious and have a good business sense (I think they are stupid and they are bullys).

I siad I wanted to be a pet store owner (I decided at last). Suzy siad she wanted to be a vet and treat sick animals and she siad that she can treat the sick pets that I sell. Miss linda siad what a good idea it will be if we work together as a business (I think that is a very good idea and this way suzy and me will be friends for ever even after we grow up and finish school). Alot of the girls want to get married and have babys! Miss linda siad they can get married and have babys and have a career too when they grow up.

A new girl in our class who came today in the middle of the term her name is Sumaya siad she wanted to be a univercity professor and when miss linda asked her what you want to teach she siad philosophy. Miss linda siad she was very impressed.

I like sumaya and suzy likes her too. The two inventors (Saleem and Ahmad) thought that teaching philosophy and becoming a professor is a waste of time and they laughed at sumaya (this is why I think they are stupid and bullys).

Suzy told sumaya that if she came a few days earlier then she would have been invited to suzy's birthday but she didn't she came today 😞

I siad to suzy is it ok if I give sumaya my mirror

and comb set from the birthday? Suzy siad it's ok and it will make sumaya feel better because she looks sad. So I did and sumaya siad thank you and then suzy and me decided that sumaya will become our friend.

Best thing that happened to me today:

1. I made a new friend ☺

2. Daddy siad that at the end of this term we are going to Aqaba!!! Yes!!!!!!

☺☺☺

CHAPTER 18

1

Khaled asks me to get the door. I hesitate for a split second before slipping off the kitchen stool, which causes him to look at me nervously.

"You promised, Nuha," he chides.

"Cool it. Everything will go splendidly." I try to put more optimism in my voice than I feel.

I open the door. He is holding a potted plant in his hands, a shy smile on his lips, and, to my surprise, he appears a little self-conscious. Clearly, Khaled had the talk with him, and I'm certain Khaled had explained the ramification of what would happen if tonight's get-together went south.

I, to put it mildly, do not like this guy. But I promised Khaled, and that's a promise I'm going to keep.

"Lovely, thank you." I take the plant from his outstretched hands and usher him in. "Please come in. Make yourself comfortable."

Trying to play nice. What bullshit! But evidently, we both love Khaled enough to make this whole charade work. Then, even before he sits down and while Khaled is still in the kitchen and out of earshot, he goes and utters the most bizarre thing to come out of his mouth since the first day I ever set eyes on him. "I may have denied it or tried to hide it in the past, but I envy you, Nuha," he says, then pauses for a few seconds to search for the right words. "I love Khaled, but you know his soul. You know what he thinks before he does. Sometimes when I look at you two, I wish he and I had the same level of understanding." He looks at me imploringly, searching my face for understanding. I do understand. He turns, and I, flabbergasted, look at his receding back as he goes and finds a seat.

Khaled's argument from a few weeks ago comes back to me. *'He is jealous, Nuha! Can't you see that?! Don't you realize he sees us together and begrudges what we have? He doesn't get us. He doesn't understand how we work together.'* And just like that, I take this man's words as an apology for every past misdemeanor.

2

Ibrahim is his name; a telecommunication specialist is his profession, a keep-fit-fanatic is his aspiration—but as far as my interest in him goes, he's my husband's lover. However, Khaled disagrees with that designation. He once explained that a mere lover offensively diminishes what Ibrahim means to him. It talks about only one aspect, that word, and leaves out all others. Three years ago, Ibrahim became Khaled's partner in the gym project, and a few months later, he advanced to more than a business partner. In Khaled's words, Ibrahim is his inspiration and creative muse.

I first met Ibrahim face-to-face weeks after hearing his name mentioned several times a day. The meeting occurred at the new gym's opening night, an event I would never have dreamed of attending if not for Khaled. He would have been crushed if I didn't make an appearance, and understandably so. It would be a cause of great speculation if one's wife didn't attend the opening of one's darling project. So, on my first and last appearance at *Musclelaneous*, and against all my reservations and rules, Khaled drove me the distance outside my usual routes, and there I was introduced to Khaled's new business partner. About five minutes after the introduction, however, it became clear to me that Ibrahim was more than Khaled's business partner and friend, or at least, very soon would surpass being merely a friend if he hadn't already.

The turnout at the opening would have made any new excited owner proud. I looked with pleasure at my husband, beaming and making the rounds, pointing out new equipment, handing out flyers, and gesturing to the posters that adorned the walls.

While guests were mingling and nibbling on small cakes and *petits fours*, and while speeches were being made by the new proud owners, Tea was stuffing her mouth with confectionery and snickering to Areej that after all this carb intake, Muscle*laneous* owed free memberships to the attendees of this gathering to help them lose the calories that they consumed by attending.

Areej, however, was not giving much heed to Tea and was instead concentrating on her Khaled. To say that Areej adored her only son would have to be an understatement. From my knowledge of the relationship between mother and son, she literally lived for him. Over the years, Areej had received many offers of marriage from well-respected gentlemen of her acquaintances. Into her sixties, Areej still exuded confidence and good breeding, but she never remarried, although she never tires of repeating that she always dreamed of a large family. Since the divorce, she devoted herself to her small family of two, dreaming of the day Khaled married and gave her the large family she always coveted.

Therefore, the idea that Khaled was gay didn't fit her plans. He, of course, tacitly understood this and so had never told her or even hinted at it. Naturally, there must have been telltale signs over the years; either Khaled hid them well or Areej noticed but decided not to acknowledge them.

Throughout university and many years after that, Khaled kept up the pretense that he would tell her soon, any day now when the time was right. His biggest fear was that she would be hurt and think she had failed him somehow. 'You know how it is, Nona?' he used to ask me rhetorically, not waiting for a reply. 'I will tell her when the time is right.' He kept on repeating over and over and never doing the deed.

Finally, as the years passed, I stopped trying to convince him otherwise. I stopped telling him, 'It's ok, Khaled,' and 'You are a great person, Khaled,' and 'She loves you, Khaled, and will accept you as you are.' And in return, I stopped hearing, 'I will tell her soon, Nuha...,' '...tomorrow,' '...in a month,' '...after she comes back from her trip,' '...the time is just not right...,' '...after graduation,' '...after I find a job.'

It never happened, and I'm starting to think it never will. For all his remarkable attributes and courageousness in confronting all his career obstacles and making a name for himself, when it comes to the most basic need—for him to be comfortable in his own skin and be proud of it—Khaled is a coward.

3

The smell wafting from the kitchen is making my stomach grumble. I sit with Ibrahim in the living room and look at him while he's sifting through our DVD collection. I know he already knows the title of every DVD in that stack. He's just distracting himself so as not to make small talk. I cannot blame him, if I have to be honest.

And yet, I want to talk to him, to say something, anything. I owe Khaled as much. I rack my brain in search of a safe topic. The Muscle*laneous* is the only thing that comes to mind and is the safest.

"So, how's work going?" I ask with all the cheerfulness that I can muster, but sounding flat all the same.

"Very promising up until our last video chat, but we'll know more when we're there on their turf," Ibrahim answers me absently while reading the back of the DVD case in his hand. "I'm optimistic. We both are, actually," he adds emphatically, this time placing the DVD back on its shelf and looking at me.

The look of horror on his face when he sees my perplexed

reaction is genuine. There is no way it's staged. He openly doesn't know that I have no idea what he is talking about. Ibrahim stands up with confusion on his face and takes a step toward me, but then stops and directs his attention to my husband, who saves him from having to explain by choosing that exact moment to enter.

The smile on Khaled's face dims fractionally when he senses the mood in the room, but Ibrahim shoots him a question before he has a chance to react. "You didn't tell her about the Dubai venture?"

There is no accusation in Ibrahim's tone, just guileless surprise at Khaled's omission. Khaled is visibly flustered at this sudden and unexpected turn of events, and although I'm piqued at having been left out of what is unfurling to be a life-changing event, I cannot but feel sorry for him as I witness his discomfort and frantic search for words.

"With Mama unwell and everything else, Khaled must not have found a good time for such important news, I guess," I say with a smile in Khaled's direction, cutting all further discussion on the subject. I see the emotion on his face, with guilt, relief, and maybe a hint of gratitude in the mix. But what irks me is not that he failed to tell me. It's something that goes deeper than that. When did our paths start to diverge, Khaled's and mine? I thought I took most of the responsibility for our recent swerve, but now it appears that we share it equally. Both of us had other things on our minds, and we failed to connect for a while. Sadness has been my default setting for a long time, but this fact, the fact that Khaled and I are drifting apart, pierces my heart. However, I promise myself that not this or worse will make me lose my cool tonight.

4

Khaled's stuffed chicken vanishes in less than a quarter of the time it took to make it. The three of us linger around the table with promises of dessert, chitchatting on nothing and everything, except the one subject I want to know more about but will never ask. Definitely not in front of Ibrahim, that is.

The ominous outcome of this gathering that I had previously predicted does not come to be. Ibrahim is a transformed man as far as I can tell, yet I don't know how much of this transformation is a scripted act and how much of it is genuine. The subject of the Dubai venture has yet to be renewed in open discussion. Still, it looms over our three heads like a guillotine threatening to glide at any moment.

Dessert is an apple pie with ice cream on the side, both made from scratch by our esteemed chef. The goodness of each mouthful is almost enough for me to forgive him and let it slide. However, I won't forgive him, and I keep a stronghold on my resentment, albeit well-hidden, all through the evening. While we make our way to the living room, more chatter on the brilliance of the cook and comments on how none of us can eat another bite and so forth follows. Khaled asks if we're up for coffee or tea. I decline but suggest that I make them both whatever they want and slip into the kitchen for a short reverie.

Indistinct voices come from the adjacent room. My head is pounding, and I have precisely zero interest in knowing what they are whispering about. I just want this evening to be over. Then, finally, I hear my name, and Khaled calls me back. "No need for the tea, *habibti*. Ibrahim is just leaving."

I grudgingly go back to them to see Ibrahim at the door, scowling. He notices me, smiles apologetically, and waves. Seconds later, the front door closes after him, and I see Khaled rest his back against the door, head bent, staring at his feet as if in defeat.

"I did not tell you because there was nothing to tell yet. I wanted to make sure there was something worthwhile to say before I said it," he says with a clear and strong voice, yet still eyeing his feet.

"I don't care," I say firmly and with resolve. My reply takes him by surprise. Of course, he is not expecting that. So, I will make myself understood without vagueness or trite remarks. "I don't care that you didn't tell me about Dubai, so don't try to explain why you didn't. However, I care that I have been going on and on about your unhappiness and depression for the last few months. How Ibrahim was not good enough for you, and talking about the despicable way he treats you, and you let me go on. Not once did you try to contradict me and let me really know the guy, instead you comeback with corny remarks, what was it the other day that you said? You still like what you saw in the mirror!! What shit was that?! And yet, in reality, you were planning for a future with him and planning big as I gathered tonight, and by accident, I might add!" I'm not finished, and I take a long, deep breath, determined to continue.

"Nuha, stop right there!" he interrupts me, shaking his head frantically.

I ignore him and continue, "Not once, Khaled. Not once did you come out of your room, while he was making a fool of himself in the apartment venting his anger after one of your stupid tiffs! Making me feel I need to defend you against the big bad wolf. You were right. You did give me all the ammunition to hate him, and yes, you are to blame for how I feel about him. You did nothing to dissuade it, you did nothing to change my mind; you act like you tried, but no, you didn't. You just love playing the victim."

"The victim?! Are you kidding me?!" The incredulity in his voice again fails to deter me.

"Yes, the victim! Your speech the other day did not change how I felt. You could have told me then what I know now, and you could have explained it better, but you didn't. You gave me just enough to make me feel inadequate that I couldn't understand what you were going through, but not enough to make me change my mind about Ibrahim."

"You fail to see yourself, Nuha," he says. "You fail to understand how difficult it is to talk to you. To explain things to you. I have to tiptoe around you and your feelings, afraid to hurt you. I am a victim, you say. You are the damaged porcelain doll!"

I look him up and down with all the disdain I can summon. "Oh, you've set me straight now, Khaled." The jeer in my voice is unmistakable. "*Jaban* coward!" I manage to add before I turn and walk away. I hear his footsteps following me as I head to my bedroom. "*Jaban!*" I repeat before I slam the door in his face.

5

I look at the two framed photographs on my nightstand, retrieved from their temporary residence in Big House for the night. I pick them up, one in each hand, and look closer. I say nothing; I don't cry; I do nothing but stare.

Tonight, I will have the dream again. I just feel it.

I slip under the covers in my clothes. I read the very last entry from the notebook with the dandelions. I close it and rest it beside me on the bed. I place my hand on the notebook's cover and keep it there for a long time. I want to see Zaid. I must talk to him; I need to. I stare into the darkness and wait for oblivion.

Tuesday 8 november

I am studying and studying and studying and that's why I don't write a lot in you my dear diary! But I will write in you and tell you everything I will do in Aqaba.

Yes!!! This weekend we are off to the red sea!!!

My mommy and daddy are the best mommy and daddy in the hole world. They siad we will go to aqaba and that's what we are going to do IN THREE DAYS!! ☺☺

They first siad they will take us at the end of term, then mommy told daddy lets go this weekend and again at the end of term! YAY

I asked mommy if suzy and sumaya (my 2 best friends in the world) can come but she siad that the car won't fit us all, with M and Taesar and the bags. I'm a little sad but I will bring them sea shells and a little glass bottles of colored sand that mommy siad they sell in aqaba. In summer daddy siad maybe we can ask suzy's parents and sumaya's parents if we can all go together to aqaba!

waw 😊😊 great!!!!

So it is my mission to find out all the cool places to go to and all the cool things to do in aqaba for next time.

M siad he will help me in my search for the cool stuff. I'm not sure if I will let him, but he did keep his promise to me and he really did study hard for his midterm exams so I might make an excepsion and trust him with this important misson. And it is his birthday tomorrow (he will be 7), so I will consider it part of his present from me hahaha.

Best things that happened to me today:

1. AQABA here we come

2. AQABA all weekend

3. my two best friends might come to aqaba in the summer yay yay yay

4. my mommy and my daddy are the BEST!

5. daddy said he will take us tomorrow to eat ice

cream for M birthday in a big nice hotel (but the cake and presents will be in AQABA)

Dear diary, please don't be mad but I'm not taking you with me to aqaba, because I don't want you to fall in the wrong hands (M). I will keep you safe and warm under my pillow in my bed and I will write everything when I come home, I will not forget anything. And I will write tomorrow and tell you about the ice cream and the hotel.

I promise... see you later ☺

Good Night.

CHAPTER 19

1

Gigi answers the phone on the first ring and, without pre-amble, assures me that all is well and there's nothing for me to worry about. I hear muffled voices, and then my mother's cheerful voice comes on the line. "*Sabah alkhyr* good morning!"

What I predicted came to be; I had the dream. I was all alone on the beach, and even the dog didn't come. I woke up drenched in a cold sweat, as cold as the water around my feet in the dream. But my mother's bright exclamation on the phone warms me up.

"Good morning to you too. How are you feeling today?" I ask.

"I'm better now," she says, emphasizing the word 'now.' Meaning that she's better when she hears from me. A statement that should make me feel good but always manages to accentuate my failings. I want to ask about her night, but she beats me with her own question. "How was your dinner last evening?"

"It was good," I say. "Khaled's chicken was delicious. Not one bite left."

"How was your friend? Did he come with his family?" she asks.

"No, Mama. Ibrahim came alone. He is a divorcé, actually."

What follows is the mandatory question that always follows when my mother hears of someone who is divorced. "Does he have children?"

"Yes, a girl. She's five and lives with her mother," I answer.

"*Yal masakeen* poor things," she retorts.

My mother doesn't know, and won't understand even if she did, that Ibrahim and his ex are so much better off now than they would have been if they had stayed together.

"You sound great this morning, Mama. Did you have a good night's rest?" I ask, changing the subject.

"Yes, I did. I woke up only once during the night," she answers. "Gigi was a pain, though. Treating me like a baby."

"I'm sure she means well, Mama."

"Hmm," she responds. Something was troubling her, and it wasn't Gigi. "*Habibti*, I feel a lot better today, and I know you've been neglecting The Place. So please go there today; don't come to Big House."

I feel a stab of guilt at her words because that is precisely what is going through my mind. However, I am not as eager to go to The Place as I am desperate to see Zaid and talk to him.

"I will try to pass by this evening, Mama. Take care, and if you need anything, call me, or let Gigi do it. Promise?" I ask.

"Promise," she replies.

2

The apartment is deserted when I leave my room. He didn't even make coffee, but he had spent the night in his bed, which I see still unmade when I peek in. A feeling of unease creeps upon me; messy is not a trait I would ascribe to my husband. I'm not sure why I care about his personality attributes at this moment, but I do. I should be mad at him now, but I am not, and that disturbs me even more. Trying to untangle my feelings now will only manage to tangle them further, so I abandon the idea.

I decide to pass by The Place and call Zaid from there. Saja is watering the plants when I come in. "You're early," she comments without looking my way.

"You're earlier than me, and good morning to you, too," I say.

She turns to me suddenly and looks me up and down. "You look quite nice this morning. What's the occasion?"

I didn't sleep all that well, and I don't feel 'nice' in any way, but I thank her as I make my way to my desk, where a pile of boxes waits beside my chair.

"They came in yesterday when you were off work, just like the day before yesterday." I hear Saja's snippy tone from behind me.

I ignore her latest pitch and busy myself with opening the boxes and assorting the contents into stacks to go on the shelves. Minutes pass, and then I ask Saja to help me arrange the books into their respective stands.

"I'm busy," she retorts.

"With what?!" I snap back at her. I'm angry now. I thought that Tea would end Saja's newly acquired insolence, but Tea's efforts don't seem to have been effective.

Saja gives me a once-over, but something in her demeanor changes. It's as if she finally understands that she's crossing a line.

However, I don't give her time to respond and deliver what I have meant to say for some time now. "Your disrespectful attitude has recently reached new levels, Saja. And although I don't know why (false statement, I do) nor do I care (true statement, I don't), I do care that employees of mine adopt a friendly demeanor as I have to spend most of my waking hours here. So, cut it out or find another place of employment."

In less than an hour, we arrange the new books. I check my emails and answer a few, make a couple of phone calls to sellers, and bid farewell to Saja on my way out. I might have to spend most of my waking hours in The Place. However, I'm spending the rest of today's hours with Zaid.

Out on the street, I fetch my phone and dial his number.

"*Galbi* sweetheart," he answers.

I tell him what I want. He tells me to come over. So, I do.

3

I'm naked on his bed. He lies beside me, propped on his elbow, gazing down at me. His eyes like coals, black with desire. His gaze is so intense; the longer he looks at my nakedness, the more brazen I feel. I am totally exposed. I want to open my soul for him, and I want him to see every crevice, expose every cell, and read every secret. His stare at my most intimate places intensifies, further igniting a fire deep inside my core. I feel liquid heat spreading from my center and pooling between my legs. I want his touch desperately, but he likes to play by his rules, and I know him well enough to realize that when he's in this mood, asking verbally will not do. My eyes silently beg.

I feel his fingers begin to caress the trail seared by his burning eyes moments before. His fingers become motionless when they reach my most sensitive spot, just applying pressure. He doesn't move. My hips involuntarily start to move and rub against them, and he lets me. His eyes bore into mine.

I gasp when I suddenly sense his fingers start to make agonizingly slow sliding movements. One stroke, two, and then a third time, and as abruptly as they begin, they still again, and his fingers shift away from my center, leaving me bereft.

He positions himself between my legs. His eyes are still on mine. I moan with pleasure; I want him inside me, but I know that's still far away. So I have learned to be patient.

Full of desire, his eyes leave mine and travel down my body again. But I still do not feel a touch. I am desperate now. I am tortured; I hurt from the lack of contact. I ache for his caress. He blows lightly on my skin; my immediate response is a moan. I want more. I feel his stubble. He moves his chin on my sensitized skin, slow at first, then quicker, lightly at first, and then rougher. I inhale audibly, and a sob escapes me, and then I sense his tongue where his fingers were minutes ago—light, feathery licks. I want to move closer, be closer to his tongue, and feel more of him. He knows what I want; he senses my need but doesn't comply. Instead, his hands tightly grip my thighs, inhibiting any advance.

He increases the pressure of his tongue, and I moan appreciatively. Tiny, light bites followed by tender licks. When he bites hard, I groan. I can hear and sense the rhythm of his breathing. It is getting wilder and harsher. I feel his tongue slide inside me, exploring and surveying my folds. It dives deeper, and I feel it move in circles as if excavating my insides. The feeling is exquisite. It is a pain mixed with pleasure, blended with ecstasy.

My hands fly down to his head, holding on to it for dear life; my fingers play with his hair, urging him on. And then I feel it gradually building. It starts behind the eyes, and then it grows. A high that spreads through my core and flows to my extremities. The intoxicating feeling of my climax forms where his mouth currently resides and then moves to every cell in my body. I feel myself climbing and climbing and then shudder violently. Then I fall.

Minutes, hours, or maybe eons later, I lie naked in his arms. The tips of my fingers trail lazily through the hair on his chest. His skin is warm and comforting. We say nothing for a long time. He kisses the top of my head, and his fingers languidly move through my hair. I can hear his heartbeat, even and strong; it reassures and grounds me. He traces his fingers from my breast, down my front, and further down still. His fingers hesitate. They stop moving just for an instant, as if contemplating their next move. Then, as if decided, they resume their exploration. The tip of one finger tentatively traces the almost faded, pale, flat, thin scar in the center of my lower abdomen, just above and horizontal to my pubic bone.

"You've never asked," I say.

"No," he affirms.

"How is it that you've never asked?"

Zaid doesn't say anything for a full minute and just stares

into my eyes. I can feel him searching for the words. He's as assertive as I've ever heard him when he speaks. "Because I've been planning to find a way to be with you forever. We have time. You'll tell me when you're ready to tell me."

220

Part 3

DARK PERIOD, BAD DAYS, AND BEYOND

CHAPTER 20

Sameer
April 2006

"You will learn to tolerate the pain; you will learn to control it and not let it control you. The pain is there, and it is severe, but you know how to hide it from other people. People who needn't know that you are hurting every minute of every day, people you care about and know care about you, people who hurt because you are hurting, and you don't want that for them. So, you become the world's best mask. Sometimes you might slip and show something that you know you shouldn't, but these slips become less in number and shorter in duration with time.

When your sister passed away, I felt nothing. In a sense, I was surprised by my own lack of feeling. For days, I thought that I had prepared myself well for the aftermath of what we knew was coming. In another sense, I was proud of this accomplishment. That I was strong and had what it took to withstand this crisis and take charge. Oh, how wrong I was! No one can prepare oneself for a ridiculous loss.

For weeks or even months, I don't know, I lost track of time then, I thought I had things under control. I felt that if I kept my feelings under wraps, everyone else would understand. There was no need to talk about it. What was there to talk about anyway?! But I was wrong, Nona... I mean Nuha. I'm sorry, habibti, I forgot, my brain isn't what it used to be, my dear. I was mistaken, Nuha. I needed to talk, I needed to vent, I needed to share, and I should have. One must not make a tragedy crueler by causing another one to occur. But at the time, this kind of simple reasoning escaped me.

It's alright if you don't want to talk to me, Nuha. It's ok. But I hope you hear what I say. I want you to listen to my words, habibti. I worry about you all the time. Night and day, I feel you. So if you want me to stop talking, I will. Tell me to stop if you wish to, and I will, but not for long. I will come back, and I will sit with you, and I will talk, and you will have to listen or tell me to shut up again, and again I will. But I will keep coming back again and again."

"You know what your mother told me the other day? She said that she saw you smile! She told me that she was so happy that she wanted to come and hug you, but was afraid that you would stop smiling if she did.

It is ok to smile, habibti. I know. I know. Don't look at me like that. I understand, Nuha. I can even guess what made you smile. You remembered. You remembered something they said or something one of them did. You remembered, and that's what makes it bearable. If bearable is the right word, but I can't think of another.

Your mother loves you, Nuha, so much.

People may think that the more we remember, the more unbearable our life will be. I disagree. I think the more we remember, the prouder we are of our contribution to this world. The prouder we are that we brought something so wonderful, talented, and funny into this world. As short as their time may have been in this life, that does not diminish its importance. My Faten used to love to plant things. She would always keep the fruit seeds she ate to scatter them later. You would always find seeds in her pockets. She usually sprinkled them here, around Big House. You know the lemon tree at the back?? That was Faten's. Oh, I've already told you that? Ok, ok, my dear. My brain is muddled these days, habibti. Forgive an old man. Anyway, what I wanted to say is... what did I want to say? Yes, yes. Whenever I remember this, I want to say that I smile, and when I see the lemon tree and the palm tree at the front of the house, I smile. All the time. This is what remains, the good and the funny memories. Don't cry, habibti. Don't cry. Ok. I'll stop talking now..."

CHAPTER 21

Roqaya
April 2006

"*Tetek ta'baneh kteer, your grandmother is so tired, my dear. I've been tired for so long. I'm too old and too exhausted. I should have been put to rest long ago. I am ready. But Allah has other plans for me, it seems. Come here and put your head on my lap, Nuha, habibti. Like you used to do when you were little, and I used to sing you that song... That's right, habibti, that's right. Do you want me to comb your hair? What was that song? I don't remember all the words... oh, no, wait...*

Yala tnam yala tnam wa'ahdilak tayr alhamam
Rwh ya hamam la tsadeq beghani la Nuha tatnam[*]

Do you remember that, Nuha? You sleep if you want. Or if you want to talk, I will listen. Or if you want to cry, you can. If you don't want to do anything at all, you also can.

You know what your grandfather Allah yerhamo, may Allah rest his soul, used to say? He used to say: 'ahyanan min 'akbar alne'am 'ala al'insan alnesyan, sometimes one of the greatest blessings is forgetfulness. He is right, you know, if not for forgetfulness, life would be unbearable. And yet, here I am cursed and a hundred years old. I am cursed! I remember everything and everyone and every word. I wish I didn't, but I do. Your grandfather used to laugh and say: Roqaya thakertek methl alfil, *your memory is like that of an elephant!*

Did I tell you about Sameer's brother? The baby I miscarried when I was only twenty. It was before I had your aunt Sameera Allah yerhamha. Yes, he was my only other boy besides your father, and I was so

---

[*] A traditional lullaby sung to children to put them to sleep (Palestine and the Levant).

young and naïve at the time, and then after him, all your aunts came tumbling one after the other. I still cry for him, you know. And there was another girl between your aunts Sameera and Muneera Allah yer-hamhom. I wanted to name her Basma, and your grandfather wanted Salwa. But, in the end, she was neither. She was tiny and weak, and she was only two days old when she died in my arms. I still remember her as Basma though, and it makes me smile, just like the meaning of her name. And now, Sameera, Muneera, and Mona. Three of my grown daughters all dead. Dead before their ailing elderly mother. And here I am with the memories and the aching frail body.

Why am I telling you all this, you ask? I really don't know… I know it's not the same, that what happened to you is not the same. I see that, habibti… Maybe I just want you to know that no one thinks you should forget. Those few people that say 'you will soon forget' are mistaken; they may mean well, but they are wrong. You should never forget. But with time, remembering will become different. The memories will become less painful, but you will never forget them.

I know, my baby, I know. You can cry all you want, but it will change. Even if now you don't feel that it could ever change, it will. Look at your father, habibti. He never forgot his Faten or loved her any less than the first day he held her in his arms. At first, he might have felt that his life was over, but things changed with time. Finally, he was able to love again, as strongly and as deeply as his first love, he loves you, Nuha, so unbelievably much…"

CHAPTER 22

Sarah
May 2006

"Nuha, my love, your landlord called again. I don't know what to tell him. Your father and I are at a loss. Tell me what you want us to do. It's been months, habibti. Your father has been paying the rent and will keep on doing it as long as you want...do you want him to? Think about it, you don't have to decide now, take your time, take as long as you want, there's no rush..."

"The dog has been pining for you, Nuha. Yes, he misses all of them, I know, but he misses you too, don't shut him out, my love. He sits outside your door almost all the time. I have to drag him for his walks sometimes. Do you want me to let him in? Or, how about you take him for his evening walk? Maybe you'd like that, love... some fresh air..."

"Well, how about that?! I should have suggested that walk a long time ago. It's ok, sweetie, that you didn't go far. That's ok, at least you breathed fresh air. Look at that dog, he is ecstatic! Let him in, Nuha. He is grieving, too. Dogs feel pain and loss. I heard that they could help. You two can help each other, habibti. Look at him! It's as if he was waiting for an opening to wiggle himself through. He's already on the bed and over your legs! Ok, sweetie, I'll leave him if that's what you want. You'll walk him every day too?! That's great. Just great, Nona baby... I mean Nuha... I'm sorry, sweetie, old habits die hard..."

"How about I make your favorite today? Musakhan?!*

---

* Musakhan: A Palestinian Arab cuisine dish. Made of roasted chicken cooked in onions, sumac, and other spices, served on taboon bread and covered by fried pine nuts.

Nuha, you have to eat. This is not right. You can't keep on like this. I know, honey, you don't feel hungry, but you have to try, a little bit, for me.

Of course I know how you feel, honey! To tell me that I don't understand what you're going through is so unfair, Nuha. I am grieving too. I lost something precious too. What happened was a catastrophe. I loved them and doted on them. And now I am left crushed, but to see you wither away in front of my eyes is torture. That I can't do anything to help you is agony. I can't see you like this and leave you alone, but that doesn't mean that what happened didn't break my heart too."

CHAPTER 23

Sameer
June 2006

"Nuha, your mother tells me that you want to go to your old apartment, and I want you to know that I wouldn't mind keeping a hold on it for you for the rest of my life and then some. You just say the word, and the rent will be paid in full every month. So you needn't feel pressured to go now.

Ok, honey, if that's what you want. But you understand that it's been empty all this time, and we only went there once to get the dog and a few things for you. So maybe your mother and Gigi could go first and give it a once-over... No? Ok, as you wish, habibti, but are you sure you want to be there alone? I could go with you...? Ok, as you wish..."

"What happened, habibti? Tell me, please. Your mother is frantic. She's beside herself. She, I mean we, the both of us, can't see you like this weeping all the time and... hysterical... Honey, what is it? How can we help? Please! What can we do...? Nuha, I won't keep from you that we've been seriously considering consulting a professional. I know you said you don't want to see anyone or talk to anyone, but... I don't know what to do.

Ok, no professionals, no doctors of any kind, but you must open up and tell us what happened in the apartment to make you so distraught? I know, Nuha, what you're going through; I know it all too well. But something new has happened, I'm sure of it. I knew I shouldn't have let you go all alone to the apartment; I should have insisted. Ehki la baba, habibti, tell Daddy, my love."

"What's this notebook you've been reading? Can I take a look, habibti? I've seen you hug it lately. What is it? What do you call this

"

flower? This one, the one that you blow on and make a wish? Yes, a dandelion, that's right. Whose pretty notebook is this with a dandelion on the cover? Oh! It was your Faten's notebook, I see...

I still remember that day in the hospital when you made us grandparents at long last. How happy we were! We brought at least fifty pink balloons with us, your mother and I. Mahmood was over the moon, his parents were already there, and we added our pink balloons to their pink balloons, but your room wasn't large enough! And then Mahmood couldn't keep it in any longer and had to tell us your surprise. The surprise you both decided on the same day you found out you were having a girl. You wanted to surprise me, and you sure did. I was the happiest and the proudest grandfather. I couldn't hold in my tears when you told me that you decided to honor the memory of her late aunt and call her Faten."

"Come here, my love... You can cry on my shoulder. It's ok, it's ok. I know, I promise you I do, you don't have to say a word, I understand. It's ok to cry. I'm going to tell you the truth, Nuha, and you need to listen to me carefully and try to understand: It will not get less painful, but with time, it'll become different; it will become another type of painful. It will become easier to handle..."

CHAPTER 24

Khaled
2012

"I have the solution to our collective problems! Just listen to me till the end. I have rerun this speech in my mind a thousand times, and I don't need any interruption, Nuha, ok?"

"Nuha, it's a win-win solution. Think about it. I get you, and you get me; we feel each other, we understand each other. I need a change, and you need it too, and we can do this together. You'll get all the well-wishers, all the Nuha-you're-still-young people, and all the Nuha-you-can-start-over people off your back. For all intents and purposes, you'll be starting anew, and as for myself, oh my God! I need to get out of the rut I'm in. I love my mother to bits, but I cannot live like this anymore, I have to get out, or she'll smother me. The other day, I mentioned in passing the idea of getting my own place, and she went into hysterics. And by the way, one more girl she wants me to get to know and marry, and I might jump off the roof. So think about it, ok?"

"I know, habibti. But it's not like we're moving to the moon. We'll be a few minutes by car. We'll find a place close to all your spots, Big House, my mother, and The Place.

Nuha... we both need this, and I know what you're thinking, I know... I will tell her soon but now is just not the right time... and even if Areej knew, and even if everyone knew... you'd never find someone who loves you more than I do...

Now, that's the smile I was aiming for... are you on board, sunshine?

YES! That's what I want to hear... I'll arrange everything, and by the way... as far as proposals go, did you ever imagine one as romantic? Ouch! You don't have to pinch..."

CHAPTER 25

Nuha
December 14th, 2017

"You've never asked… you have noticed it, and I saw you more than once touch it with your fingertips, but you never asked me about my scar, not once, Zaid. I would have told you if you had asked, but you never did. Your total lack of curiosity stunned me, to be honest. I didn't understand it initially, but now I think I do. We are so close, yet you respect my boundaries, and thank you for that.

Zaid, 'us together forever' is just not… I'm not saying I haven't suspected you were thinking about it, but this is the first time you've voiced it. There are things you need to know about me, honey. I want to tell you now. I want you to know… everything."

"No, Zaid, please let me talk. I want to do this, I want you to hear me, and I want you to feel me. I want you to finally understand me. Understand why, although we are as close together as any two people can be, I still keep you at arm's length. Understand why, although you want more, I can't give more. And although I have noticed you hinting at it, I can't be to you more than I am now. I know that you love me. I know that with all my heart. In the beginning, I didn't grasp the depth of your feelings, they didn't make sense to me, but now I do understand, and they do make sense, and this is in part why I want to tell you what I'm about to. The other reason I decided to open up is that I realize it's unfair what I'm doing to you. Keeping you suspended, not knowing, hoping, no resolution in sight. What's the phrase? Yes… in limbo…

Promise not to interrupt me, habibi, please. I'm going to get it out, here and now. I'd rather it be the easy way, not the hard way. I don't want to fight with you. I don't want this to be an argument. I just want you to hear me out till the end...

Remember once you asked me why I didn't use a profile picture on WhatsApp before the one I have now? Remember?

Yes. Well, it's true, I never did before, and if it wasn't for meeting you and what meeting you awakened in me, I wouldn't have. Why? Because, to put it mildly, I don't like what I see when I look at myself. Or maybe I didn't used to—recently, something has changed. You certainly have a lot to do with it, but other people in my life have also contributed to this change. Like Khaled, for example... oh yes, Zaid, we're going to talk about him today too."

"This scar here, this is a cesarean scar. This was my second born, Muawiya. My first was my Faten; I had her the old-fashioned way. I see the look in your eyes, Zaid, and know you must have suspected. Anyway, you'll soon understand everything... just hear me till the end.

I was so young when I had them. I had barely graduated college when Mahmood and I got married. I don't know what happens to girls at that age! Most of us, except the lucky few, get the wedding fever. It was very contagious that year, the marriage madness that is. I remember five of my close friends, including myself, got married within two months that summer. All of us convinced that we had found our soulmates and that we were madly in love.

Anyway, where was I? Yes, we had my Faten a year later. My beautiful girl was a little over a year old and had just started to speak when we had Muawiya, whose name was a little too much for Faten to pronounce correctly, so one thing led to another, and Faten decided that his name will be M and so it stuck, and in no time even his grandparents and everyone we knew was calling him M.

Mahmood was a good guy, kind and generous, not my soulmate by a long shot, I now realize, but back then, I was too young and inexperienced to even know what soulmate really meant, so it was easy to play content and happy. But we were happy in a way, with the babies mostly. They were the center of our lives. All grandparents doted on them and on us because deep down, they knew that their offspring were actually too young and inexperienced for the responsibilities of married life and needed a hand, so you see, we weren't faking our contentment. But, of course, you could say we were immature and didn't know better, and we had our babies so early on that we didn't have time to think better of it, and life rolled on.

Khaled was the only person who thought I was crazy to be getting married while not yet twenty-two.

Yes, Zaid, I can see your surprise, and yes, I knew Khaled back then. I knew Khaled years before I got to know Mahmood even. Khaled was my best friend all through university, and well, he still is my best friend, I guess. Oh, don't look at me like that. He is! But that's neither here nor there. I'm not leaving here today until everything is out in the open and you see the whole picture.

Khaled didn't particularly warm up to Mahmood. Although they weren't frank enemies, they weren't friendly either. And that was the main reason, I guess, that our friendship, Khaled's and mine, cooled off at the time. I wasn't going to let anyone, not even my best confidant, stand in my way of wearing white, having a wedding, inviting my friends and family, and playing house. All the idiocy that girls with the wedding fever affliction think will make their lives complete.

Mahmood and I were lucky in that we both found jobs right after graduation and had a stable income, and like I already told you, our parents helped us a lot, so we were, at least, financially secure. The other thing that helped our marriage to 'work' was our babies. We lived for them and rarely allowed ourselves to think outside of their orbit.

Our sex life... well, I didn't love it, that's for sure. But honestly, what can an inexperienced girl, who hasn't been properly kissed before marrying, actually know about it or compare it to? You see, Zaid, here's the thing, I have only ever had sex with two people, Mahmood and you.

You know the emoji with an 'O' for a mouth? You look like it right now. But I need your undivided attention if I'm going to do this and get it all off my chest tonight, so snap out of it. Are you with me? Ok then...

So, let me just reiterate that you two are the only people I've ever slept with, and up until I got to know you, I thought that I knew what it was to be intimate with a man. But, it turns out, for all intents and purposes, I was still a virgin despite the two children!

When I saw you that first time in The Place, a feeling that I have never felt before—and this is not an exaggeration—stirred inside me. A magnetic pull to a man I see for the first time yet feels so familiar. I don't know how to explain it! I've never met you, but I knew you. I felt you. When you enter a room, everything else disappears; you are all that is left, all that matters. I know that you understand what I'm saying because not too long ago, you explained to me how it was for you the first time you set eyes on me, remember? It was more or less the same for me. You touched a place in me that is raw and pristine. You made me want things I hadn't wanted for a long time and never thought I would again.

The sequence of events that led us here today, you and me, was meant to happen. I feel it. I know it now. I'd always thought that the term soulmate was so clichéd. When I heard it repeated, as it so often was, I felt it to be a timeworn, overused expression. But when I saw you, it fit into place. It started to make sense. How could I be so drawn to this person that I don't know and have never met in my whole life? It was the only explanation I could summon at that moment.

But even after all this, I honestly had no idea you would come to feel for me like you do now. When I realized the adoration you held for me, it was too late. I needed you and still need you. You made me feel. You made me feel again! I couldn't imagine anyone could love me this much. I know Khaled loves me, but this, what we have, what you give me... this passion and devotion... This is new.

Which makes it all the harder for me to tell you that we, you and I, can't keep going on like this, the way we are now. I realize that now, so clearly. I must tell you everything. I must clarify, and then you can decide. It's unfair what I am doing to you now. You say you love me, and I know you mean it, but love alone will not compensate for the things that staying with me will deprive you of. Even if you might think that love is enough now, I don't think that holds true in the long run..."

"No, Zaid, this is not about Khaled. It's about us. The two of us and why we can't continue as we are now without you first understanding things about me. And it has nothing to do with Khaled. But this is as good a time as any, I guess, to tell you about Khaled.

Ok, I've known him since forever, my Khaled. And he's, you might say, my, that word again, soulmate. Or one of them, I suppose. It's nothing like what you and I share. It's different.

Khaled knows the nitty-gritty of my soul. We have an understanding between us that few appreciate. He helped me through the years in ways that even my family couldn't or wouldn't have known how to.

Anyway, Khaled saved me from me; he gave me a new purpose, and he always grounds me if and when the need arises. He is a generous, compassionate person, one of the best people you could ever meet. By the way, Khaled knows about us, Zaid. He's known since the beginning or soon after. His reaction two days ago was solely because he doesn't want our marriage to crumble. It's too important to him that we remain married. He knows what you mean to me... He only wants me to be more careful. I can see your shock, Zaid. But let me explain...

Khaled has his own issues that he struggles with, such as self-confidence. You see, simply put, Khaled is homosexual. I've known from our very early beginnings. I was one of the very few friends that Khaled confided in back then, and now it's sad to say that all these years later, not more than a handful of people know the truth. He feels he needs to hide it, does it well, and always finds new reasons why he shouldn't just come out, many of which are rooted in social and cultural concerns, as well as personal reasons that I will not delve into at this time. He was the one to come up with the idea of us getting married, and I have to confess that the plan benefited both of us when he proposed it, and it still does to this day. There is a certain security to marriage, especially one like ours, the well-thought-out union of convenience. Still, in the beginning, I thought it was my duty to try and sway his resolve and encourage him to come out and live his life freely, but it seems that my heart wasn't into it, and in the end, I quickly capitulated because I needed to get out of Big House.

Ultimately, I'm trying to say that Khaled is a big part of my life and an essential one at that, but he is not the main reason for my tell-all to you today."

"Today is about a part of my past, a pivotal time, a period that I refer to as my 'bad period.' An event that skewed my life off its course.

Like I told you earlier, Zaid. I knew that you were thinking of finding a way for us to be together always. Even if I only heard it voiced today, I felt it. I knew that sooner or later, you would start hinting at the subject and then try to convince me to see it from your point of view. You will never quit, even if I find excuses and a rebuttal of every argument. You will try it over and over again.

But, habibi, what you're asking is ludicrous. It's illogical, and I could never do that to you. For us to be together, for us to get married is unreasonable. It's ridiculous. I'm sorry, but it is, Zaid!

Please don't look at me like that and hear me out. You are still young. You'll marry someone closer to your age, and you'll have a family. The age difference will make us a standing joke, the object of ridicule of all Amman. And even if we're to turn a deaf ear to the whispers, your mother and sisters will have a fit, and probably you will lose them forever. And even if by a miracle you managed to convince them to accept me—and that is a big IF!—I can't give you what I know you want. Ok, let me rephrase that. It's not that I can't as much as I won't. The idea is abhorrent to me. My whole being revolts at the thought...

You see, Zaid, once upon a time, I had a family, and I don't want another one. I had my babies, and I don't want to have more. I know that you think this is negotiable. But I am here to tell you that it is not!

I know you love me, and you think because of that love, you can surmount any obstacle, but you can't, baby. You just can't...and I don't want to see the love in your eyes turn into bitterness. You will resent me one day, and I can't have that, Zaid.

My family was taken from me. There we were one minute with dreams and plans, good times and fights and... everything. And in another minute, it was over. I had nothing; I was all alone. My two babies perished instantly, I was told later. They also said that Mahmood died on his way to the hospital. They told me that he was calling 'Nona, Nona,' over and over. He was searching for me, that was my name back then, but not anymore... Nona ceased after that day...

What followed is what I call my 'bad period.' Years of self-loathing. I was inconsolable. Almost catatonic. I refused any kind of therapy. More out of defiance and stubbornness than anything else.

A couple of days ago, I told you we moved to Big House because my grandmother was getting older and weaker, but that wasn't the whole truth. The main reason was me. My parents decided to move me to Big House and nearer to my grandmother because I had a solid connection with that woman, and they thought she could help. It was a comfort to be near her. It helped maybe... a little...

The bookshop helped me to start wanting to wake up in the mornings again, but that came years later. Khaled then rescued me and took me out of Big House. Much as I like that house, I was in a rut while in it, and leaving it and making my own sanctuary somewhere different helped me move along.

And then... and then this dark stranger entered my life and blew up all the walls I had up to protect me... That passion! That adoration! I had no chance...

And now here we are, my love, telling you all this so you can understand that despite all your love for me... no, no... that's not right. Let me rephrase... Because of all your love for me, I can't continue to delude you with false hope...

Give me a moment. I swore to myself I wouldn't get this emotional, but it's just not possible. Even after twelve years, it still cuts to the quick...

Just hold me..."

Zaid hugs me tight. A shudder of terror runs through my body at the memory of that day. The day that spared me while it should not have. I still think of the audacity of life; twelve years have passed, and I still can't get over it, as if it happened yesterday. No, not yesterday—minutes ago, seconds even. My father was correct; it didn't get less painful. Instead, the pain transformed into a dull, deep ache that burrows into every cell. It lingers and persists and resists every kind of penance or act of atonement.

I feel Zaid's hand slide up my naked back and cup the nape of my neck, pulling me closer to him. I sense his warmth, his warm breath caresses the top of my head, I smell his familiar scent, and I feel his safe presence. I feel him; I know what he's thinking. He still doesn't grasp the cruelty of the situation. He still thinks there's a negotiation after this, and he still has a chance to convince me of his point of view. I know that's what he's thinking or something along those lines. If it was any other person on any other day, my mask would be securely on by now. But today, the mask is nowhere to be found and will stay off. He doesn't utter a word per my request, but I feel him loosen his embrace. He looks into my eyes and waits.

"Yes, Zaid, yes, I know that look, I've seen that look before, the one you're giving me now, and I've heard it all, believe me! Of course, you're assuming that what happened must have been an accident of some sort. That it's not my fault, that there was nothing I could have done to prevent it. But it doesn't feel like that to me. I should have died with them!

I know I will keep going, that I will not give up. I thought about ending it all. I was close to trying it once; I came close to taking my own life, but I didn't, and now I promise you that I never will.

You see, something happened to ensure that I'll never try to end my life again. This was months after, and I hadn't been to our home since the day I lost them. When I eventually gathered the guts to go there, I found something under my Faten's pillow. It was her diary; I gave it to her on her birthday and asked her to write in English to improve her writing skills, and write in it she did, my darling girl. I had forgotten all about it, and when I found it and realized what it was, I was about to go mad with grief and seriously thought about ending it all there and then. But instead, that diary has become the thin thread that ties me to this world. It is what keeps me hanging and trying to find a reason for living...

It's been twelve years, one month, and five days today... I keep count, you see. They were taken from me on my M's seventh birthday. On his birthday! I know that's when I should have left this world too, but I didn't, and until this day, I don't understand why my life was taken from me and why I am forced to stay here to only exist. I try to make sense of it, but it always eludes me. The reason, the purpose of my existence... I don't see it, Zaid. But I will keep searching...

Four thousand, four hundred, and eighteen days... that's how many days are in twelve years, one month, and five days; I keep count of the days too...

We were out to get ice cream, and Mahmood had promised Faten to take us to a fancy hotel, and we always kept our promises to them, always. They were waiting for me in the lobby when it happened. I had to use the restroom, and I left them there. Faten had asked me, do you want me to come with you, Mommy? And I asked, do you need to go? And she said, no, I just want to keep you company... And I stupidly, foolishly said, stay with Daddy and M, I'll only be a minute... And a few minutes later, I heard and felt the blast. I should have been with them. I shouldn't have left them on their own... I will never forgive myself that I had. NEVER!"

And still, true to his word, Zaid doesn't speak and waits for me to finish. Perhaps my expression conveyed a warning that contributed to his ongoing silence. I look into his eyes; they look back at me but are blank, unfocused. He is listening to my words; it's clear that the word 'blast' didn't sit well with him. He's trying to understand, trying to focus, but failing. He doesn't make the connection; why should he? Why would he, or anyone, for that matter? He was so young when it happened, barely out of school. My grandmother used to say 'Alnysayan ne'ma min Allah,' forgetting is a grace from God. Humans forget; they can carry on because of this blessing. Catastrophic events are not wiped but put aside, hidden away, and stored in our memories to be retrieved only in cases of necessity. Only those who lived through them or had their lives annihilated by them, but by some miracle only just held on to their sanity, will start counting years, months, and days.

"My boy would have been nineteen last month," I tell Zaid. "He was born on the ninth of November." I stop talking for a few seconds. Remembering. Getting tormented by the memories.

Zaid tilts his head and looks inquisitively at me. I can almost see the lines of data in his thinking process. Memory blocks being taken out of storage, dusted, and washed for inspection.

Twelve years, one month, and five days later, it is still hard to say the words, but I do. "They all died in the 2005 Amman bombings*."

And just like magic, Zaid's eyes focus, and I register the shock on his countenance and the sorrow that always follows.

---

* 2005 Amman bombings: Organized suicide bomb attacks on three hotels in Amman, Jordan—The Grand Hyatt, the Radisson SAS, and the Days Inn—on the 9th of November, 2005. The attacks were claimed by the Jihadist Al-Qaeda in Iraq organization, killing sixty people and injuring one hundred and fifteen.

CHAPTER 26

1

My mother passed away on the 16th of April, 2018. She went peacefully in her sleep. Gigi was the one who found her; Mama had been feeling better for a week or so, and I wasn't with her that night. It happened one hundred and twenty-three days after Zaid and I parted ways, and one hundred and twenty-four days after my fallout with Khaled.

After sharing my story, I planned for Zaid to make an informed decision about us, understand my limitations and what I could and couldn't give him, and start thinking about a future—if not immediately, eventually—without me in it. Still, after that long and heart-wrenching discussion, it became clear that whatsoever my story was, his mind couldn't or wouldn't conjure a scenario that did not include us together forever as a family crushing hurdles and overcoming every barrier in our way.

Zaid was precisely what I needed when I met him; I was everything he didn't need. So we had to end. I stopped picking up his calls or returning his messages. He tried to explain and make compromises for me, and although my soul felt empty and my body bereft of pleasure after we parted ways, my conscience wouldn't allow me to complicate his life any more than I already had. Zaid cannot see it now, but soon I will be a memory, a good memory maybe, but still a thing of the past.

We've patched things up, Khaled and I, as we ultimately always do; it's just how we are. His hugs were enough to soothe me after Mama. He asked me once about Zaid. I couldn't find the words to articulate the void Zaid's exit left in my soul;

honestly, I didn't have the energy to search for them. So, I just told him I had to let him go for his own good. Maybe it was the timing, recent events, or possibly both. Still, regardless, neither of us seemed inclined to talk it over nor explore it further.

2

Today, five months after Mama's passing, I stand on the shore, looking at the stretch of the Red Sea* in front of me. I wanted to hike the Appalachian Trail and even started the process of applying for a United States visa. I told Khaled, and he said that it was a fantastic idea but suggested baby steps first. I had to admit he did have a point, which at long last led me to Aqaba instead. Khaled had a last-minute change of plans and couldn't accompany me. He had to travel to Dubai because their deal, his and Ibrahim's, was finally going through. I'm happy for him, I really am, and I wish him all the success he deserves. In fact, I'm pleased for both of them; maybe some time away from me will do them good. However, Khaled told me that Ibrahim is planning to reside in Dubai, while he, Khaled, will travel back and forth. Secretly, I rejoiced; I can't ever bear the thought of Khaled not being in my life.

I went to Big House to bid farewell to my aunts before I took this trip. They didn't acknowledge that it was my first time out of Amman in a very long time and what such a step signified for me. That didn't bother me; my aunts have been living in their own jolly universe for as long as I can remember, and I, of all people, can't judge them for it. However, they chastised me for not including them in my plans and complained that they never go anywhere. And made me promise

---

* Red Sea: Name is a direct translation from Greek: Erytha (Red) Thalassa (Sea). A hypothesis about the origin of the name is that the algae *Trichodesmium erythraeum*, upon dying, turns the sea a reddish-brown color.

to bring back souvenirs, and to take them the next time I go, and to include Khaled in the trip. Of course, I promised, or they would've never let me hear the end of it.

On my way out, I saw Gigi. "Take care of them, Gigi," I said.

"*Bieuyuni*," she replied in Arabic. Gigi has been with us for so long and I knew well enough that the phrase *bieuyunni* is a solemn oath to keep them safe, as if with her *'eyes.'*

"*Allah yesalem euynek*," I said. "God bless you. I'll be back soon, Gigi."

"I know you will, Nuha," she said. Gigi has transcended being the hired help a long time ago. She is family now, as close to me as a sister. So, I said no more and squeezed her into a hug.

3

The cool water laps around my bare feet, and I feel the pleasant sea breeze tickle my face and tousle my hair. This was the trip that we should have taken almost thirteen years ago, but didn't. So, I can finally say now that my life has come full circle.

There is a dark side to me, and many might call me callous. But it's not true; I can love and be loved but sometimes don't show affection like others. I have experienced different loves in my lifetime. Love is not just one kind; there are several.

The love of a parent is unmistakable; it's unquestionable care. My parents would have gladly given their lives if they could spare me pain and suffering, and I would have done the same for my children.

I have experienced the love of a soulmate. One who feels what I feel. Who can soothe me out of a tempest with a touch. Who knows when to press and when to ease. Who knows where the lines are drawn, when to step and when to stop. Who knows my sore spots and the amount of pressure needed, when to put it on and when to pull it away.

I have also experienced the all-consuming love of passion, the earth-shattering love. The kind that blows the mind away.

Today, I stand here to commemorate the loves of my life. I want to prove to them, as well as to myself, that their love is appreciated and honored. Being alive today is a testament that their love mattered and still matters, that their lives mattered and still matter even if they are no longer in earthly form. Those of my loves that are not with me in body today are, in fact, buried deep into my soul.

Baba and Mama, I love you so much and always will. I am sorry for the heartache I caused you, and I hope you know that I didn't plan to take your love for granted, but that's how it was during a significant part of my life. You gave, and I took. You supported, and I benefited. And for that, I am eternally grateful.

Grandmother Roqaya, you wise and amazing woman! Your brand of tough love, even in my darkest hours, helped to give me stability and calm. Even if I didn't show it then, I am thankful to have known a pillar of strength such as yourself.

Khaled, my person and best friend, you held my hand and wouldn't let me fall even when I begged you to let go.

Zaid, you were my refuge. Your passion gave me strength; I could have conquered mountains in your embrace. Your adoration taught me I am worthy of love and can start loving myself again. In the end, your respect for my wishes is a testament to your honorable character.

My friend Tea, you tolerated my tantrums and childish behavior, never complained, and never gave up on me. You are my rock and my inspiration.

Faten and Muawiya, the apples of my eye and the loves of my life, you were the best kids any mommy could wish for. I honor your existence on this earth, short as it was, by staying alive even after you departed it and remembering you and your kind and loving father every day until my last day. I promise you, my loves, that I will find ways to go on until we meet again.

I'm reminded of one of the perks of working in a bookstore. The riffling through books at random and the reading of snippets, some of which are lost to you after seconds of reading them and others that linger because they tug at a string you never knew you had. Verses by Robert Frost that I read not too long ago echo in my mind now:

> *The woods are lovely, dark and deep,*
> *But I have promises to keep,*
> *And miles to go before I sleep,*
> *And miles to go before I sleep.*

I am not afraid.

EPILOGUE

February 2022

A bright pink letter 'N' balloon catches my eye as I quickly scroll through my Facebook feed. I swiftly backtrack two posts, and there it is—a picture of a large helium-filled letter 'N' posted two hours ago.

I'm completely mesmerized by it. My gaze is locked on the screen, and although I can identify the post's author, I'm still struggling to connect him with the message typically conveyed by pink balloons.

It had slipped my mind that Zaid and I were friends on Facebook. As I recall, he has never posted, and today marks the first time seeing his profile picture in my feed, leading me to believe that whatever it is, it is monumental.

My eyes blur, and it takes a moment for me to realize that there are tears in my eyes. But these are good tears, happy even.

Oh, my Zaid! I'm so happy for you, but I won't tell you that. You'll have to believe in your heart that I do and always will. Like I once told you years ago, I'll one day be a memory, hopefully, a good memory. And today, you proved me right.

The photo announces the arrival of a new baby girl—Nuha.

ABOUT ATMOSPHERE PRESS

Founded in 2015, Atmosphere Press was built on the principles of Honesty, Transparency, Professionalism, Kindness, and Making Your Book Awesome. As an ethical and author-friendly hybrid press, we stay true to that founding mission today.

If you're a reader, enter our giveaway for a free book here:

SCAN TO ENTER
BOOK GIVEAWAY

If you're a writer, submit your manuscript for consideration here:

SCAN TO SUBMIT
MANUSCRIPT

And always feel free to visit Atmosphere Press and our authors online at atmospherepress.com. See you there soon!

ABOUT THE AUTHOR

DIMA BADER, a dentist by profession and a storyteller at heart, was born and raised in Amman, Jordan. She now lives in Long Island, New York. This is her first novel.